THE LIPSTICK CIRCUS

The Lipstick Circus

by

BRIAN McCABE

O 91494/5-

MAINSTREAM
P U B L I S H I N G

First Published in 1985 by
MAINSTREAM PUBLISHING COMPANY (EDINBURGH) LTD.
7 Albany Street
Edinburgh EH1 3UG

The publisher gratefully acknowledges the financial assistance of the
Scottish Arts Council in the publication of this volume.

McCabe, Brian
    The lipstick circus : and other stories.
    I. Title
    823'.914[F]   PR6063.A13/

    ISBN 0-906391-87-3
    ISBN 0-906391-88-1 Pbk

Typeset in 12 point Van Dijck by Studioscope in conjunction with
Mainstream Publishing.
Printed by Butler & Tanner, Frome, Somerset.

Contents

Acknowledgements

Some of these stories have been previously published in
*Firebird 1, The Glasgow Magazine, New Edinburgh Review, New
Writing Scotland 1 & 2, The Panther Book of Scottish Short Stories,
Scottish Short Stories 1979, 80, 81, 82, 84 & 85, Sharp Edges* and
Stand.
'The Full Moon', 'The Sunbather', 'The Lipstick Circus' &
'Hiss' were produced for radio by Patrick Rayner and
broadcast by BBC Radio 3 & Radio 4. 'A Little Bit of Repartee'
was broadcast as part of Radio 3's Scottish Season 1984 and
was produced by James Runcie.

FOR DILYS

The Sunbather

HE HAD SEEN her there every day, in the same place beyond the rocks, a little away from the main stretch of beach. Clearly she had chosen the spot with care — it allowed her enough privacy to discard the lower half of her black bikini as well as the top. To get to it she had to pick her way over the high, jagged rocks, then follow a winding goat-track through the bushes and down to the little cove. Already she had an allover suntan as deep and as rich as anyone could wish for, but every day she was back again: stretched out on a long white towel with a red stripe, stuck to her shadow like a slim brown lizard. He'd guessed that she must be an American girl — even from a distance he could see that her heavy blonde hair was obsessively well-groomed. Every time she changed her position, which she did with monotonous regularity, she would brush the hair over and over, then arrange it so that it was perfect. On the few occasions when he had actually seen her going into the water — not to swim, of course, but simply to cool down — he'd noticed that she always tied the hair up first and took great care to avoid getting it wet. The thick blonde hair, the black bikini, the suntan, the narrow waist, the languid walk — it was all a cliche, of course. He had seen it so many times before in holiday brochures, films and colour supplements. Once, squatting among the rocks high above her and wishing he had brought his binoculars, he'd watched her shaking out that golden hair as she walked from the shallow water up to her little crescent of sand, and for a moment it had seemed as if he were watching an advertisement. There was nothing original about her then, yet he found himself scaling the rocks each day to watch from above, and though he didn't actually try to conceal his presence, he didn't make a point of being conspicuous either, but moved silently to his vantage point as an atheist might tiptoe into the rear of a church.

He didn't enjoy sunbathing himself. His fair skin burned and blistered too easily, and he had that underdeveloped kind of body which looks so awkward and vulnerable in beachwear. He had come to the island with a different purpose in mind, bringing with him a bag heavy with paints, drawing materials and even a fold-out easel. He was after all a trained painter, and had just finished his first year of teaching in a Comprehensive in Surrey, but so far he had done nothing apart from one or two stylised sketches, unworthy of an 'O-level', of the lemon trees outside his hotel window. He tended to spend the afternoons in the tavernas, stunned by the heat and unable to order his thoughts, drinking beer after beer until it was time to think about dinner. Though he hated to admit it to himself, and had given no indication of it in the one post-card he'd managed to write but not send, he was bored with being on holiday. Perhaps this was why he took an idle interest in the sunbather — far from bored, she seemed perfectly at ease, in her element. The fact that she was always alone on that little fingernail of sand somehow enhanced this. As he watched her change position, or bow her head to tie up the hair, or apply more oil to her long brown thighs, the word which always came to his mind was *devout*. Perhaps he was also intrigued to find that the illusion, this creature of the brochure and the screen, really did exist in life. In any case his idle interest soon grew into a fascination, and he found himself longing to go down to the cove and lie there on the sand beside her. He found it difficult to foresee any kind of conversation — what do you talk about to a completely naked stranger? — but imagined it pictorially: the gently undulating horizon of that long brown body against the luminous blue sky. Perhaps a single cumulus cloud suspended above her, its shadow falling on her breast. Surrealism, in his experience, could be all right if the subject was suitable for that kind of treatment. He wished he had brought his oils.

He became so preoccupied with the sunbather that one afternoon, even though the sky was completely overcast, he struggled over the rocks as usual in the hope of finding her there in the cove. When it was clear that she wasn't there, he sat down and waited hopelessly, telling himself that if she came by he wouldn't hesitate to speak to her. Certainly he'd introduce himself, strike up a conversation, maybe invite her to go for a beer. He imagined her blue eyes — he hadn't actually seen them, of course, but felt sure that they would be as blue and immaculate as the sky had been until today — gazing into his over a candle-lit dinner. The elegant brown Modigliani of her shape against the white walls of his hotel room. His hand following the contour of her neck and shoulder, feeling the texture of that brushed blonde hair. The fact that she wasn't there and, he knew deep down, wasn't liable to appear on such a cloudy day, allowed his fantasy to accelerate as he waited, sweating and itching in his thick cotton shirt and cut-off jeans. The air was heavy and humid —surely it must rain or thunder soon, surely something must transpire. When the images crowding into his mind began to insult even his own sense of what was credible — surrealism was surrealism, but life was life —he picked up his bag and sketch-pad and made his way back to the beach. There were a few people sitting on the beach in groups of three or more. Half a dozen men were playing with a frisbee, and as he walked passed them he eyed their tanned, well-proportioned bodies — would she even consider being seen alongside a pinkish, freckled, narrow body such as his? As he turned to walk up the beach, the frisbee whirred past his head, so close that it made his ear tingle. One or two of the men laughed, and a dark-haired girl who lay on the sand nearby reading a book looked up at him over the rims of her glasses. He felt himself flush as he passed her. He hurried on to the village, where he stepped into the dark cool of the first taverna he came to. The waiter was a boy of eleven or twelve who looked, in his white shirt and black waistcoat, like a miniature adult. He came over to the table and wiped it and said yes. Feeling the need to get a little drunk, he ordered a metaxa with his beer. He watched as the little waiter — perhaps he was older than he seemed? —poured his drinks and brought them to the table, carrying the tray on one hand just as if he had been doing the job for decades. Already he had that air of deliberated boredom of the professional waiter. He thanked him and gulped noisily at the beer, then laid the sketch-pad on the table and opened it. He had taken it out with him in the hope of doing something — a sketch of the sunbather, even from a distance, would be better than nothing — and now he doodled on the blank pages as he drank. He found himself trying to draw her from memory, but with each attempt it became clearer that he hadn't seen her closely enough. The figurines which resulted were imaginative in the worst sense. The first attempts were crude versions of a brochure photograph, with the blonde goddess stepping out of a badly-scribbled sea. The drawings degenerated as he drank, the last being little better than dirty drawings.

He was staring at the doorway when a girl stepped through it, tossed her rolled-up towel on to his table and collapsed into a seat opposite him.

'Mind if I join you?' she said. She leaned back in the seat and yawned, but her brown eyes magnified by the glasses looked wide open and eager for contact.

Recognising her as the girl who had witnessed the frisbee incident, he flushed and stammered that of course he didn't. The waiter came over and said yes, with that look which said I've seen it all before. As she ordered a beer, some bread and feta, black olives, he looked at her closely for the first time. She had straight black hair, still wet from the sea, which clung to either side of her head like treacle, dividing to expose two large pink ears. She had a wide, straight mouth which opened into a grin as she spoke to the little waiter. Her body wasn't exactly ideal, being more like two bodies joined at the waist — the top half small and thin despite the wide hips and heavy thighs — but she was not unattractive. And there was the wide-eyed eagerness about her despite the slovenly way she sat — as if she saw her own body as an encumbrance, so much unnecessary luggage. The voice too was a curious mixture of laziness and impatience as she asked him where he was from, and what he did, how long he had been on the island, as if she wanted to get these boring preliminaries out of the way as soon as possible so that they could talk about something important.

'I teach too,' she said, 'in the heart of darkest Manchester. As you can imagine it isn't quite the prime of Miss Jean Brodie. More like the breakdown of civilisation as we know it. On a daily basis, that is. Still, I won't bore you with my repertoire of anecdotes, all that classroom violence and staffroom intrigue and exam futility, all those little things sent to try us in our struggle to spread the word. We're on holiday, after all, although in my case it's more a convalescence but still.' She spoke in a flat, bored tone, but the words came quickly to her. He listened to her and smiled and said nothing, moving around restlessly in his seat. 'Mind if I have a look?' she said, her hand already on the sketch-pad. He did not want her to open it, but felt unable to say no.

'They're doodles,' he said, 'a waste of paper.' She opened the pad and began turning it this way and that. The waiter brought her beer and the food she had ordered. She popped an olive into her mouth, cut a slice of the feta and laid it on a piece of bread. She jammed this between her teeth and, taking a wide bite, began chewing energetically. After a moment she gulped at her beer and flicked a page of the sketch-pad over.

'Who's this,' she said, 'Miss World?' She stabbed at the darkly pencilled buttocks with a finger. 'I wish I had muscle-tone like that! Not likely with my figure. Not at this rate anyway — they smother everything in olive oil here.' She held up the bread and cheese to show him that it had indeed been dressed with olive oil, then pointed again to the sketch. 'Who's the centre-page spread?'

'It's nobody,' he said, 'no one I know, just a doodle.'

'Quite a shapely doodle,' she said, taking another olive and spitting the stone into her hand. 'If you did know her you'd be lying there beside her I'll bet.' She was pointing to another of the drawings, in which the impossibly long-legged sunbather lay stretched out on the sand.

'Maybe I would,' he said, forcing a smile.

She poured more beer from the bottle into her glass and said: 'Along with a few hundred others.' She went on to talk between mouthfuls as she flicked through the sketch-pad — he could tell she found the drawings amusing and pitiful — about how overcrowded the beach was, how she'd never believe another brochure-blurb in her life, how she'd come to the island for peace and quiet. Of course she'd wanted to meet one or two interesting people, but so far had come across only the usual 'loud men without brains' like the ones playing frisbee on the beach. Those, and then the hateful middle-aged British couples intent on having chips with their moussaka. With a kind of bored indignation she told him that in three days she hadn't met a single person she could have an intelligent conversation with. He pretended disbelief — he'd been on the island three weeks and hadn't had any conversations, intelligent or otherwise. He nodded and smiled as she talked, but his three weeks of silence and solitude felt like a heavy weight inside him, dragging him down. He had to force the words out one by one — it was an effort even to ask her where she was staying.

'Alexandros,' she said, making the name into a yawn, 'same as you. I'm on the ground floor at the back, room nine. Come down one evening if you like. I've got a bottle of duty-free cognac. I could show you some of *my* drawings.'

'How did you know I'm staying there?' he asked.

'I saw you at dinner the other night. You're in the upstairs part, are you? Which room is it?'

'Eighteen,' he said, at the same time wondering why he felt so reluctant to tell her his room number. 'So you've been doing some drawing here too?'

She told him about the drawings she had been doing. Nothing serious really, just quick things of the old women in their black shawls, the men leading their donkeys, the children playing in the village square, and then the one or two abstract things, in which she wanted to capture something of the island's atmosphere . . . She began to talk more generally about art in relation to experience, and he sensed that a long discussion on aesthetics would soon be underway if he didn't interrupt.

'Maybe I'll come down then, see what you've been doing.' He drank the last of his metaxa quickly and stood up.

'Are you off now?' she said. For the first time there was a note of surprise in her voice.

'I think I'll get back to the hotel now,' he said, 'have a siesta.' She shrugged and popped another olive into her mouth. As she chewed on it she looked at him steadily, and the look in her large eyes seemed to be saying, why are you running away just when we're getting started? Before he left she asked him his name and told him that hers was Barbara. And it was with a feeling of escape that he stepped out of the taverna into the bright glare of the street, though when he asked himself why this should be so, why he hadn't at least suggested that they meet for dinner, he couldn't say.

Later that night in his hotel room, after eating a congealed slab of moussaka in a dreary little taverna at the far end of the village, he fell on the bed and thought of going down to room nine. What was wrong with her, after all? She was intelligent, friendly and even attractive in an individual sort of way — so why not? Even if they didn't actually have what is called a holiday romance — and wasn't that, watercolours or not, what he'd really come looking for? — they might spend some time together usefully, even enjoyably. All he had to do was get up, shower and change, then go down to room nine. Instead he drowsed and dreamt of the sunbather: blonde, suntanned, perfect, she was stepping from behind a screen — one of those screens the models had undressed behind at art college — and she was wearing that black bikini, so brief that it merely emphasized the features it concealed. There was sand all over the studio floor, and among the many easels and deck-chairs the students were sitting talking and smoking cigarettes, or lying in attitudes of catatonic collapse. All were dressed in shorts or swimsuits because of the heat, determined to find a good space of sand in this overcrowded studio and set himself up before the model was posed — but where was the model? He caught a glimpse of her towel with the stripe disappearing through the studio door. He hoisted the easel —unfortunately it was the cumbersome art college kind, not his little fold-out one — and staggered through the studio with it on his back. A frisbee whirred past his ear and somebody laughed derisively. Someone else jeered behind his back, shouting something about Christ on his way to Calvary, and then he was through the door and in a long corridor of light. He picked his way precariously over the rocks, past the college cafeteria and down to the cove. He could see her down there, spreading out the towel and kneeling down — could she be praying? — and already she was unfastening the top of her bikini. In his hurry to get down to her, he slipped on a loose rock and the easel swung from his grip. In wonder he watched it bounce and leap and tumble over the rocks, at last plummeting down to land upside-down in the sand. There it stood, the image of a primitive gallows. He ran down the goat-track, shouting to the sunbather and waving a hog's-hair, square-headed brush in his hand, and at last he was approaching that slender brown back. When she turned around, he woke up with a gasp.

The days became less clearly defined, ran into each other as the sky ran into the sea. It had rained often and the sky had become more or less permanently overcast. There had been no sign of the sunbather anywhere. What did she do when it rained? The question intrigued him more than it should have. Every day he made his little pilgrimage to the cove, and every day he was disappointed. Every day, too, he had seen the treacle-haired Barbara in and around the hotel. His own reaction to her puzzled him. Though she had more than once come over to him and begun a conversation, he had responded as stiffly as a Presbyterian minister to her suggestions and invitations. But then this was of no real importance. What mattered was that he was in love — he felt sure that this was no delusion — with the stranger he'd seen enacting her daily ritual, communing with the sun down in the cove. One thing which had continued to trouble him, however, was the climax to that dream: when she had turned to face him, why had his subconscious seen fit to substitute Barbara's bespectacled eyes, her wide grinning mouth and even the black roots of her hair showing through the blonde?

One morning he awoke to find that outside his window the birds were singing in the lemon trees, and above them the sky was a cloudless blue vault. Thanking God aloud, though he was no believer, he swore to himself that this time, if given the chance, he would not hesitate. He would use every trick and tactic he knew to make his fantasy real. In the intervening days he had planned it: when she arrived at the cove he'd already be there, in a little place he'd found under an overhang. That way she wouldn't be able to see him from above and be put off by the presence of a stranger in her little sanctuary. She'd catch sight of him only when she reached the foot of the goat-track, and then he'd look up and say hello. He'd be sitting there working on a drawing, of course —he'd already done one or two stylish things of the rocks around there and Barbara had found them quite impressive — and if his prayers were answered she'd be intrigued enough to come and have a look. He knew from tiresome experience how far people were sometimes prepared to go out of their way just to peer over his shoulder when he worked outside. If that failed, he could always ask her if she might be interested in posing for a few sketches. He was a trained artist, after all, and if he knew anything about figure-conscious American girls, he knew that she would be flattered. Even if she didn't agree to pose, such an invitation would surely be less obvious, less crude than the usual conversational gambits. He felt confident that he could take it from there.

Going over this plan in his mind, he showered quickly and packed the drawing things in his bag. Deciding to skip breakfast — he could always take her for lunch somewhere — he hurried downstairs and stepped into the bright glare of the street. As he came to the end of the village, he entered a small tourist shop on impulse. If he was going to be sunbathing with her, he should have a tasteful pair of shades and some Ambre Solaire. He chose a pair of sunglasses from the display-rack, walked up to the counter and then saw her: the white towel with the red stripe hung from her shoulder-bag. Over the black bikini she wore a full-length transparent beach-gown. The blonde hair had been tied up in a pony tail with a scarf, and he noticed that the roots were dark. For a moment she had her back to him as she paid for whatever she was buying and waited for her change, but even so he felt with sudden certainty that he had made some great mistake. When she turned round he almost laughed — not at her, but at his own foolishness: she was fifty, over fifty, probably approaching sixty. The loose skin of her neck was creased and gnarled and furrowed. To make things worse, when she turned she bumped into him, apologised in a hard, tense, American voice — he'd been right about something — then smiled at him enticingly. Had she seen him there, high above her in the rocks, the distant admirer? The grimly smiling, heavily made-up face was a taut mask of distress and anxiety. He stepped back in fright, stuttering apologies. Devout was not the word — she was fanatical: it was etched into the deep lines at the corners of her mouth, around the eyes, across the brow . . . the desperation of a woman to stay young, attractive, fashionable. It shone in her hard blue eyes like a mirage. When she had gone, he paid for the sunglasses and dropped them into his bag, thinking vaguely that the purchase was appropriate given his blindness.

It was late in the afternoon when he locked his room door and went down to room nine. He knocked quietly, but no one answered. He tried again later that night and again the next morning. When he made enquiries to the old man behind the hotel desk about an English girl called Barbara, black hair and brown eyes, wears glasses, staying in room nine, the old man grinned and with his hands made the shape of a buxom woman in the air. Then he told him that she had left the previous morning, to visit one of the other islands before going home. When he asked the old man which island, the old man scratched his armpit, sighed, stuck out his lower lip and said, 'To Crete maybe, maybe to Rhodes.' He could not, of course, say which.

The Lipstick Circus

HE FELT IT there behind him when he turned round to pick up the poker from the fender, felt its hot breath on his neck. He turned round again as quick as he could, then stood holding the heavy poker in both hands. Maybe the poker would stop it coming out, maybe it would be scared of the poker. And standing with your back to the fire meant it couldn't get behind you the way it always tried to. But maybe it could come out of the fireplace, out of the fire. He could hear the fire behind him, hear the hiss of the coal. It sounded like his father breathing, and sometimes it made another noise that sounded like his father coughing. And when the fire sparked, that was like his father when he was angry. Maybe it couldn't come out of the fire, but it could come out of anything else. It could come out of the television now that the circus was finished and there was nothing on. It could come out of the setee or the chair. Maybe it could even come out of the china cabinet with the glass doors and the little golden key, where his mother kept the things he couldn't touch. There were cups and saucers with pink flowers on them and she kept them in the china cabinet because they came from China and they were too good. He didn't think it could come out of good things with pink flowers on them, but maybe it could even although it was bad.

It only tried to come out when he was on his own in the house like this. His mother wasn't back from her work yet, and his father had gone out to put on a horse. His father slept in the morning just now because he was on the night shift at the pit, and sometimes when he woke up he went out to put on a horse. He had cried for his father to take him out with him, but his father had told him to sit there and watch the circus until his mother came home. But now the circus was finished, and his mother wasn't home. He could feel the fire getting hotter on his back, and the poker felt heavier and heavier. Maybe it could come out of that picture of the blue lady on the wall above the sideboard, out of her big black

18

eyes. And grab the poker out of his hands and . . . Suddenly the fire made a loud cracking noise, like the lion tamer's whip, and something sharp burned into the back of his leg. It was only a spark of hot coal, but he started crying anyway because it gave him a fright and he dropped the poker on the floor. He kept his back to the fire so that it couldn't slip behind him, and soon he couldn't feel the hurt place on his leg. But he kept on crying because maybe it would hear the crying and not come out, maybe it was scared of crying. But maybe it wasn't, maybe it would still come out. Out of the blue lady's eyes or maybe even out of the poker. Maybe it could even come out of the mirror with the wooden frame and the stand. He looked over to where the mirror stood, on top of the sideboard under the picture of the blue lady. But he didn't think it could come out of the mirror, because he had heard his mother saying it was a good mirror. It might not come out of the good mirror or the good cups with the pink flowers, but it might come out of the poker. He stopped the crying a bit and looked at the poker on the floor. It had a long brass handle, and a thicker part at the end that was black from the fire. It might come out of that. He jumped over the poker and ran to the setee and jumped up on to the cushions. He turned round as quick as he could, in case it had come out of the clock on the mantelpiece and was behind him. It wasn't, so he stopped crying now and ran round the setee to the big table. He pulled out one of the chairs by its back legs and dragged it over to the sideboard. One leg got caught in the carpet, and he saw the brown lino underneath. Could it come out of the cracks in the lino? He climbed up on the chair and stood looking into the good mirror.

At least now if it came out and tried to get behind him, he would see it coming. He could see nearly the whole room behind his own head, even the door into the hall. He would see it coming up behind him now unless it was smaller than him or the same size, but he knew it couldn't be. He knew that if it did come out it would be bigger than him, much bigger. He looked at his own face in the mirror. The tears were still dripping down his cheeks. He started crying again to see what it looked like, then watched himself wipe off the tears with his sleeve. Now his face was covered in snotters and dirty marks from the tears. It looked a bit like a clown's face and it made him start laughing. Maybe if he laughed it wouldn't come out at all, maybe it was scared of laughter. He laughed a bit more and watched the face in the mirror changing. The eyes were like little slits, and the cheeks swelled out like balloons, and he could see the teeth and the gums and even the tonsils. He laughed as long as he could, but after a while it started to sound like crying. It even started to hurt a bit, but that didn't matter if it stopped it coming out. Suddenly the chair wobbled and he had to grab the curved wooden back of it to stop himself falling. He didn't fall, but when he looked at the face in the mirror again it wasn't laughing any more. And it didn't look much like a clown's face really.

On the sideboard in front of the good mirror, there were some of the things he couldn't touch. There was the golden case with the little round mirror in it and the pink powder his mother put on her face. And the pencils she drew her eyebrows on with, and the pink hairbrush with hundreds of black spikes like a hedgehog. Between the spikes there were some of his mother's dark hairs. He picked up the brush and started tugging out the hairs. When he had a clump of the hairs, he put the brush down and tried to mix the hairs with his own, but when he moved his head they fell to the floor. He picked up the brush again and started brushing his own hair up at the front and the sides. It was the kind of hair that stood up when you brushed it that way, so he kept brushing it until it was all standing up on end like a clown's. This was even funnier to look at than the dirty marks, so he laughed for a long time at the face in the mirror, laughed until he could feel his eyes squeezing out two more tears. Then he picked up the little golden case he couldn't touch and opened it up and laughed even more because it looked even funnier in the little round mirror. He picked out the round piece of cloth with the powder on it and started dabbing his face with it the way he had seen his mother putting it on. He picked up some of the powder in his fingers. It felt soft, even softer than sand at the seaside, and it smelled like sweets. He took some on the tip of his tongue and tasted it, then coughed and spat the way his father sometimes did, because the powder tasted horrible. He shook the rest of it into his hair, then put the round piece of cloth back into the case and closed it.

It was good to touch the things he couldn't touch, the good things like this other golden case with the bright red lipstick inside. He pulled it open, then turned the part at the bottom that made the lipstick come out. He played at making it come out and then go in again. It was sort of like a tortoise sticking its head out then pulling it in again. Then he saw an envelope on the sideboard with the red mark of his mother's mouth on it. It was very red, but parts of it weren't. There were thin white lines through the lips, and the two lips didn't join up at the sides. He started painting the lipstick on his own lips, looking at the mouth in the mirror. He smudged it over his chin, because he couldn't help laughing at his own face with the bright red lips and sticking-up, powdery hair. When he had finished painting his mouth, he pressed his lips against the back of the envelope the way he had seen his mother doing it. The paper stuck to his lips, and this made him want to laugh even more. When he looked at the envelope, he saw the mark of his own mouth under his mother's. It looked very different. The lips were thin, and they did join up at the sides.

He threw away the envelope and looked at the face in the mirror. Now he really did look like a clown in the circus. He painted his nose with the lipstick too, then drew big black lines round his eyes with one of the pencils. There was a little jar of white cream, so he rubbed some of this on his face. He put some more lipstick on the lips, so that they bent up at the sides like a clown's. He made a funny face at the mirror and laughed again. Maybe now that he looked like a clown it wouldn't come out, maybe it was scared of clowns. But maybe it wasn't, maybe it could still come out. Out of the blue lady's big black eyes, then pull the chair from under him the way clowns did in the circus, but this time not to make anybody laugh. He looked up at the picture of the blue lady. Her face was painted too, but not like a clown's, and she was smiling but not the way a clown smiled. Her mouth sort of twisted up at one side and she had a purple flower in her hair. He had never seen anybody with a blue face, or a smile like that, or eyes as big and black as that, and he had never seen a purple flower. Maybe it could come out of the purple flower.

He put the lipstick into his pocket and climbed down off the chair, then he pushed the chair back to where it was at the table. He tried to lift it and hold it up the way the lion tamer did in the circus, but it was too heavy. He could feel it there behind him again, feel its big black eyes. He turned round as quick as he could. It wasn't there, but maybe it was faster than him, maybe it had jumped behind his back when he'd turned. He wedged himself between the table and the sideboard and stood with his back against the wall. He looked at everything in the room — the television, the fire, the setee, everything. Everything looked like it was going to move, and when he saw the clock out of the corner

of his eye it seemed to jump off the mantelpiece towards him.
When he looked at it again, it had jumped back on to the mantelpiece. Then the mirror did the same. Everything started jumping
towards him, then jumping back into place. He made a dash for
the setee and fell flat on the carpet behind it. He rolled over on his
back and stared up at the lightbulb hanging from the ceiling.
Maybe it could come out of the light, maybe its eyes were like
lightbulbs so that when you looked at them you had to look away.
He rolled over on his belly again and crawled along behind the
setee, feeling the lipstick in his pocket pressing against his leg. He
crawled to the end of the setee and felt the draught coming under
the door from the hall. Suddenly the fire made a loud cracking
noise and he jumped to his feet and ran to the door. He could feel
it there behind him as his fingers tightened round the handle and
pulled and pulled.

It was cool in the hall and quiet without the fire. He sat on the
bottom step of the stairs and looked at the coats hanging from the
hooks. One of his father's jackets was lying on the floor, under a
hook with nothing on it. His father was always throwing his jacket
at the hooks and missing, and when it fell to the floor he didn't
seem to mind. But his mother minded, because she was always
picking up the jacket and hanging it on a hook. And sometimes
she looked through the pockets of the jacket before she hung it
up, and took out the little blue slips of paper with the horses on
them. Then she took off her glasses and held them away from her
eyes, to make the writing on the blue slips look bigger. And once
when she had done this she had told him his father was a clown.
He thought about this again, but still didn't understand it. How
could his father be a clown? He didn't look like one. The only time
he looked a bit like a clown was when he came home with his face
black with the coal dust in the morning. But most mornings he
washed it off before he came home. But if he came home with the
coal dust on and smiled, then his lips looked very red — a bit like a
clown's but not really. There was another thing his mother said
that he didn't understand. She said she hoped he didn't grow up
like his father. What did it mean? Did she want him to stay the
same size? And how could he be like his father? Could he wear big
black pit boots like his father's? And throw his jacket at the hooks
and not mind when it missed and fell on the floor? And could he
have blue slips with horses on them in his pockets, and the kind of
comics his father had, with pictures in them that made his mother

curse and spit? And how could he ever yawn the way his father yawned, as if he were playing a trombone?

He jumped off the stairs and started dancing round the hall and pretending to play a trombone. He imagined the big golden trombone sliding out and in, then he remembered the lipstick and stopped. He took it out of his pocket, opened it and dabbed some of it on his finger. Then he started dancing round the hall again like a clown in the circus, laughing and playing a trombone. If he laughed loud enough maybe it wouldn't come out, maybe it would stay in the living room. When he was tired he stopped and sat down on the bottom step again. He looked up the stairs to see if it was on the landing, but it wasn't so he moved up to a higher step. Then he looked round and saw all the red spots on the walls of the hall where his fingers had touched them. He took the lipstick out again and played at making it come out and then go in again like a tortoise. Then he put his hand flat against the wall and drew round it the way his mother had shown him how to on a bit of paper. When he took his hand away there was a big red hand on the wall, bigger than his, nearly as big as his father's hand. He did the same with his other hand, then joined up the two hands with a lot of red lines. He drew in the body and the legs and the head. He drew a pointed hat on the head, then a round red nose and little slits for eyes. When he had done the clown, he moved up a step and started doing a chair, and when he had done the chair he moved up again and started doing the horses.

When the lipstick circus was nearly finished he was right up in the upstairs hall, then he heard the door opening and closing and his mother coming into the hall. He heard her shouting his name and dropping her message bag on the floor. Then he heard her screaming. The scream scared him, but not as much as being in the house on his own with it coming up behind him. He started crying a bit, because somehow he knew that she wasn't going to like the lipstick circus. She ran up the stairs, but stopped on the landing half-way up and said some of the things she said about his father's comics. Then she ran up to the top of the stairs and screamed again when she saw him. She stood there with a hand over her mouth, staring at him. It scared him to see her staring like that. He had never seen her eyes looking so big and black behind her glasses. Suddenly the lipstick flew out of his hand and his feet were off the ground. She was pulling him into the air by his arm, and her hand was smacking his legs. It hurt and made him cry, but not the way he cried when he could feel it in the room with him making the clock jump off the mantelpiece. When he was dropped to the floor, he went on crying as hard as he could, but after a while he stopped because he could hear her crying too. She was sitting on the top step crying, with the fingers of both hands in between her eyes and her glasses. He had seen her crying before, but not sitting on the top step still with her coat on. He saw the golden case with the lipstick in it and he reached for it. Maybe if he gave it back to her she would stop.

He turned over one of the big coloured pages in his new book, then picked the red crayon out of the box and started to do a clown. It was strange how they shouted at you and hit you for making a lipstick circus, then bought you a big book with coloured pages and a box of crayons and told you do another circus. A crayon circus on a page of the book was good. When he had shown the first one to his father, he had put away his comic and looked at it and had given him a shilling and said he was a future leonardo. He didn't ask his father what a leonardo was, but it sounded like the the name of a clown. And his mother had given him a biscuit and had said it was a good circus too. But a lipstick circus was bad, like the thing he felt when there was nobody else in the house. It could come out of anything. Out of the sideboard or the setee, out of the blue lady's eyes or the poker, the china cabinet or the mirror. Maybe it could even come out of him.

Anima

'HURRY UP AND make up yer mind,' said my father.

I went on staring at the dinette linoleum in silence. It wasn't yellow and it wasn't quite brown, but a sort of diarrhoea-colour in between. It was making me feel queasy, staring at it like this. I remembered my sister telling me that its pattern was called *parquet* and that it was just like Mum to buy lino that pretended to be wood. What had she meant by that? And what had she meant when she'd said that a dinette wasn't the same thing as a dining room? What was the difference? And why did we call it the dinette anyway? Nobody ate in here. Everybody ate in the living room, with the telly on and the fire. The only thing anyone ever did in the dinette was sulk. That was what it was for.

'Come *on*,' moaned my father, 'decide what to be and geez peace!'

What to be. How could I decide what to be? It had been hard enough deciding to join the cubs. Now this: what to *be*? It was cold in the dinette, but I felt strangely hot inside — hot and shivery. I pretended to look out of the window at the garden, hoping my father would go away. Then I found myself looking out at it — at the weeds and the old gas cooker and the hut made of railway sleepers. It was getting dark, and the hut looked like a little animal cowering against the wall. I noticed the packet of seeds on the windowsill, picked it up and pretended to be reading the instructions. I'd bought the seeds weeks ago and my father had promised to show me how to plant them. He'd forgotten about it though. I heard him making the most of a yawn — why did he always do that? — and I knew that he was fed up with this father-and-son routine in the dinette. He wanted to be in the living room, watching the news and arguing with the Prime Minister. Instead he'd been sent in to talk to me because I was sulking.

I glanced up at him as he yawned again. He stood just inside the door, slouched forwards like a tired old bull. His belly hung over the sagging waistband of his trousers and his braces hung

25

loose. His trousers and shirt were unbuttoned and his vest was a greyish colour. I started shaking the packet to hear the seeds. It sounded like they were whispering to each other in there.

'Come *on*. Ah've no got aa night!'

I looked at his face to see if the anger in his voice was real or just pretend. He stuck his head forward and glowered down at me in mockery, mimicking my own frown. Why wasn't he young, like other people's dads, and interested in hunting and fishing and camping and cars? Or at least in gardening? Why did my dad have to be old and tired, with thick tufts of hair sticking out of his nostrils and his ears? All he was interested in was politics and horse-racing and going to the pub. Why had my mother sent him in to talk to me? How could he help me to decide what to be? He didn't even know what it was like to be a cub.

'D'ye want to be a frogman, or what?'

That was typical. How could I be a frogman? I didn't have flippers. I didn't have goggles. Maybe the snorkel and the rubber suit could be pretended, but that wasn't enough.

I shook my head, stared at the lino and felt ill.

'How about an astronaut, then?' This time I shook my head even before I let myself begin to imagine the impossible silver suit, the helmet and the window in the front . . . 'Why no? Like Yuri Gagarin, eh?'

'How can I?' I heard my own voice whine, 'Astronauts 've got silver suits and . . . and I don't!'

'Oh ho ho,' said my father, 'oh ho ho ho ho . . .' He went on ho-hoing until it sounded almost like a real laugh, then he coughed and spluttered. 'Well, ye'll just have to be a wee monkey then, eh? That shouldnae be too hard!'

That was typical as well. All he could do was mock. He didn't understand how important it all was. As he opened the door to go out, he turned and made a face as if he was going to say something serious, which meant he was going to make a joke.

'Ach well,' he said, 'ye'll just have to go as yersel. One of the lumpen proletariat.'

What did that mean? What was the proletariat, and what had happened to its leg? As my father shut the door I threw the packet of seeds on the floor. It burst open and the tiny seeds scattered over the linoleum. They looked like insects running away when their stone has been lifted. I saw my own shadow on the floor and suddenly it looked like a giant's shadow and the hot-shivery feeling swept over me again. No, I wasn't going to be ill. If I admitted feeling ill, they wouldn't let me go at all.

I crossed the room and looked at myself in the mirror above the sideboard. Maybe I could be a pirate? But no, too many of the others would go as pirates, and their pirates would have eye-patches and cutlasses and bright, spotted neckerchiefs. My pirate would have a soot-blackened face and an old headscarf round his neck and that would be it. Too much like a real pirate, maybe. Or a cowboy? But no, somehow that was too obvious. I needed to think of something better to be, something original.

'What a fuss to make about a party,' said my sister as she came into the room. She came towards me then stood with her arms folded, staring at me. 'Right,' she said, 'you'll never get anywhere or be anybody if you can't even decide what to go as to a stupid fancy-dress party at the cubs. Turn round.'

I obeyed slowly, then stared at her elbows. This meant that I could avoid her eyes, which were too honest to look at for long without feeling guilty, and her breasts, which were too much a source of fascination and confusion.

'A pirate,' she said. I mumbled something about cutlasses and ear-rings. 'Chinaman,' she stated. I hesitated. Was it possible to be a Chinaman?

'But how could I make my eyes like a Chinaman's?' I whined, but my sister was already grasping me by both shoulders and turning me this way and that, looking me up and down, as if she could somehow tell whether or not I had the makings of a half-decent Chinaman in me.

'I'd have to use a curtain for the robe,' said my sister, 'a lamp-shade for your hat and . . . make-up for the eyes . . .' Suddenly she stopped turning me and held me still and I felt the queasy feeling again — as if I'd jumped off a spinning roundabout. 'I know what you should be!' She took a step back and clapped her hands.

'What?' I said, beginning to feel wary.

'A girl.'

A girl! Was she out of her mind? I opened my mouth to speak, but my sister got there first:

'You can wear one of my old skirts. The pink one with the zip at the back . . . We'll have to get you some stockings and high-heels — I'll teach you how to walk in them, it isn't easy — and that blouse, that cream one with the frill at the neck . . .'

I searched her eyes — *The pink one with the zip at the back!* — for some sign that she was joking — *Stockings? High-heels?* — but there was nothing — *That cream one with the frill at the neck!* — except her wide-eyed, unflinching stare. Could she be as shocked and fascinated by the idea as I was? *A girl!* My sister was out of her mind.

'They wanted a girl anyway.' She took another kirby-grip from between her teeth and pressed it into place above my ear. Her voice sounded strange because of the kirby-grips, like a ventriloquist's.

'What d'you mean, wanted a girl?'

'Instead of a boy, that's all.'

I stared into the mirror. She had stopped being me a long time ago, this creature with the thick coating of coloured grease on her cheeks, the bright red lips and darkened eyebrows. She wasn't me, but she was. Every time I spoke, her lips moved.

'Who?' I said, watching the bright lips moving in the mirror. *Who?* they seemed to be saying.

'Mum and dad,' said my sister, taking another kirby-grip from her mouth. She pressed it into place and added: 'I wish I had hair as thick as yours.'

'How d'you mean, wanted a girl instead of a boy?'

'Once they knew she was pregnant,' said my sister, standing back a moment to admire her handiwork in the mirror. 'I heard them saying they wanted it to be a girl. I wanted a sister too, you know. You came as a disappointment, I can tell you.'

'I couldn't choose what to be, could I?' I whined, staring in fascination at the bright lips. Had I said that, or had she? Was it my mouth, or hers?

'And you still can't,' said my sister. She picked up the hairbrush and began to brush the hair at the back of my head upwards. It felt all wrong.

'But that's different! Nobody can decide what to be before they get born!' I said, doubtfully. But what if people could? What if I had, and what if I'd decided wrong?

'I'm not saying anybody can. All I'm saying is you weren't what we were expecting. You weren't expected at all, if you want to know the truth. You were a mistake.'

'What d'you mean, *a mistake?*' The girl in the mirror raised her eyebrows, pouted her lips. And then the strangest thing happened — another mistake, maybe — and the girl in the mirror smiled at me. What did *she* have to smile about?

'I don't know what you're smiling at,' said my sister, 'it's true. Mum got pregnant by accident.'

By accident? I had heard different versions of how It could happen, but this was a new one on me: *by accident*.

'How do you mean?'

'I'm your big sister, am'n't I? I know things you don't, that's all. Mum and dad came up to me and they said, "How would you like to have a little sister?" Of course, I told them we couldn't afford it, but —'

'But why did they have one . . . I mean *me* . . . if you told them we . . . I mean *you* . . . couldn't afford . . . *it?*' My confusion as to what to call myself was made worse by the sight in the mirror. *It* seemed to be the best description.

'Because by that time it was *too late*. By that time she was pregnant, the damage was done.' She scattered the remaining kirby-grips on the glass-top of the dressing-table. The sound they made reminded me of the seeds scattering on the dinette linoleum and the hot, shivery feeling swept over me again . . . I imagined being a tiny insect when its stone is lifted, running away from the giant's shadow . . . Was I going to faint? (*Faint? Wasn't that what girls were supposed to do?*)

'What's the matter,' said my sister, 'don't you like it? Just the eyes to do now. Hold wide open.' She tilted my head back and began to attack my eyes with a little, evil-smelling, black brush. 'I wish I had lashes as long as yours,' she added.

'Wait till they *see*! Wait till they *see*!' My sister clapped her hands in delight and hurried out of the room. I heard her squeaks of laughter as she ran downstairs. It sounded like a balloon being rubbed the wrong way. I wanted to run and hide, but it was difficult enough to stand still in my sister's high-heels. I hobbled around the room, then something drew me back to the mirror. I sat down and looked into it the way I'd seen my mother and my sister doing it, tilting my face this way and that, touching my hair here and there with a hand. The girl in the mirror smiled, but I felt more like screaming. (*Screaming? But wasn't that what girls . . . ?*) Now that I was alone with her, she seemed more monstrous than before. She swayed towards me and smiled her eerie smile again.

And suddenly I knew what was so strange about her smile. It wasn't just that I didn't feel like smiling myself, though that was strange enough. No, the girl in the mirror was smiling *at herself*, pleased to see herself at last, smiling in triumph.

I stood up quickly and kicked off the shoes and ripped at the blouse, then the ill-feeling rose up inside me again as if I'd jumped off a roundabout. Then the world lurched and spun and all I knew was that I had to run, run because the stone had been lifted, run from the giant's shadow on the lino pretending to be wood in the dinette that wasn't the same thing as a dining room, run into the hallway where they stood at the top of the stairs, my mother with her hand flying up to her mouth letting out a whoop, my father forgetting to slouch because of what he saw with his eyes looking blue and amazed, run past them to the bathroom and the sink where I could let it all come up, hearing my father's rumbling laughter and my mother's whoops behind me and my sister's squeaking giggles like balloons, balloons with faces painted on them at the party, faces with faces painted on them at the party, faces of frogmen and astronauts and cowboys and pirates at the party, cakes and lemonade and sweets and games of musical chairs and blind-man's-buff and . . . I felt the cool hand on my burning forehead and I knew that I would never go now.

Interference

Hello.

I'm outside the door again, I can talk to you. You're not like anybody else in the class. You're from Mars, you're a Martian. That's why I can talk to you, because I'm not like anybody else in the class either. Sometimes you sit beside me don't you, when you want to ask me a question. Like what is one take away one on Earth. And I tell you the answer, nothing. Or when you want to tell me an answer, you materialize like in *Star Trek*. Just for a thousandth billionth of a second, then vanish back to Mars. Nobody sees you except me, nobody wants to. Nobody knows how to see you except me. See the dust in the air up there, where the sun's coming through the window? You're like the dust in the air — nobody notices you except me. And your voice is like interference on the radio — nobody wants to hear it except me. *You* can see everything. You can see through people, and you can see through walls. You've got X-ray eyes, that's why. I wish I had X-ray eyes. Cheerio.

Hello, come in, are you receiving me? My situation is an emergency, I have lost all contact with the *Enterprise*. I've been put outside the door again, because of my abominable behaviour. I am on the brink of disaster, and the teacher says my behaviour is detrior-hating. It means getting worse. This is an SOS. I will continue until I am rescued or until my Oxygen runs out. I'll tell you what's been happening to me down here on the planet Earth. Last week she made me sit next to the Brains. The Brains is an Earthling, species girl. With red hair, freckles and specs. I had to sit next to the Brains. She was always too hot, always wheezing and sweating, and her legs were always sticking to the seat. It was the noise I hated, the noise her legs made when she unstuck them from the seat. And she wouldn't let me use her red pencil, to colour in the sea. I know the sea's supposed to be blue *on Earth*, but on Mars it's red isn't it? And when I took that red pencil of

31

hers out of her hand and broke it, the Brains started crying. It wasn't real crying, it was a special Earthling kind of crying. Sometimes they cry outside but not inside, it's more like watering eyes. And in the middle of the crying she said something about my clothes, because I've got a patch on the back of my trousers. I can't see it, but everybody else in the class can. So I got her back in the playground. I went into the Earthling boys' toilets and I drew up some of the water, the pisswater in the pan, into my new fountain pen. Then I squirted it into her face, and it went all over her specs. And that's how I got into trouble last week, all because I got a new fountain pen. I don't like using these Earthling fountain pens much, they make too much of a fucking mess. Yesterday the teacher held my writing up for everybody in the class to look at, so they wouldn't write like me. See I don't write like anybody else, see I write in a kind of Martian. Nobody can read it except me and you, it's in code that's why. See all the mistakes are secret for something, every blot is a secret wee message. But I got into the worst trouble for squirting piss into the Brains's face. The Mad Ringmaster got me, watch out for the Mad Ringmaster. Over and out, cheerio.

Hello, come in Mars, do you read me? My position is getting more abominable by the minute. So now she makes me sit on my own, so you can sit in the seat next to me. But you shouldn't materialise like that in the class, when everybody's listening to the radio. Everybody was listening to Rhyme Time, a programme of verse for Earthling children. Everybody thought it was interference, but I knew it was your voice talking to me. And I got put outside the door again because of you. Don't try and deny it, I did. It was that poem called Spring, all about the cuckoo and whatnot. And you were asking me what that poem was all about, because there aren't any birds on Mars, are there? And I saw you out of the corner of my eye, except you kept disappearing and coming back. Materialising. When I throw a stone in a puddle, everything disappears and comes back. That's what you're like, a reflection. So I had to tell you what Spring is and what a cuckoo is, so I started making the noise a cuckoo makes. *Kookoo, kookoo* — it sounds like its name. She thought I was taking the piss out of the programme, but I wasn't. I was talking to you in the secret wee voice, the one I'm talking in now. Billy Hope, she said, this is a classroom not a home for mental defectors. Go and stand outside the door, come back in when the poetry programme's finished. But it isn't finished, because when I put my ear on the door I can hear it going on. She said it was bad enough having to put up with interference on the radio, without having to toler-hate interference from me.

I can't stand poetry anyway, it's worse than long division.

Maybe the next time you materialise, I'll use some sign-language to talk to you. I could scratch my nose for Hello. Everybody would think I was just scratching my nose. But then, if I had an itchy nose and I scratched it, maybe you'd think I was saying Hello. And if I stuck my tongue out for Cheerio, I'd get put outside the door every time I said Cheerio to you because of my abominable behaviour. I just put my ear to the door again and I heard the interference. It was you asking me another question, asking me what behaviour means. The answer is, I don't know.

I'll tell you something though: my mother's got a screw loose, has yours?

Over and out cheerio.

Hello come in are you receiving me? Listen: You were born on the same day as I was, at exactly the same time, except *you* were born on Mars. You go to a primary school on Mars, and you're in 4B like me. You're last in the class on Mars, except it's great to be last on Mars. It's like being top of the class on Earth. And 4B is better than 4A there isn't it, because everything's a reflection the other way round. You're like me the other way round. If I looked at you too much, I'd go cross-eyed like the Brains. See when you materialise in the seat that's empty, the seat next to mine —that's you doing your homework, isn't it? It's like Nature Study, except you're doing it on us the Earthlings. I bet you're glad you're not at a school on Earth. With a voice that sounds like interference, you'd get put outside the door every day. I wish you'd take me to your Martian school with you. Then I'd be top of the class — I mean last — and then *I'd* be called the Brains. We'd be first — I mean last — equal. In the Martian primary school we'd get put outside the door for coming top of the class, because that's what the prize is on Mars. On Earth it isn't a prize, nobody likes it down here. And when you're put outside the door on Mars, you can travel through space and time. You can visit other planets. Down here there's nothing to do outside the door, there's nothing to look at. Nothing except the door. And the corridor, and the clock. Earthling clocks tell the time, every tick means a second. A second, a second, a second. No it doesn't *say* it, it tells the time with its hands. No it doesn't really have *hands*, it's a machine. No it doesn't have a mind, Earthling machines don't have minds. But cuckoo clocks say the time, they say *koo-koo, koo-koo*. But birds are different from clocks. See the birds on the windowsill up there, I think they're pecking for crumbs. You should do some Nature Study on them, because there aren't any birds on Mars, are there?

Or maybe there are some birds on Mars, but they look more like cuckoo clocks. But the clocks on Mars fly round and chirp the time.

Anyway I'll tell you what to say about Earthling birds. Put down that they've got wings, beaks, claws, feathers, tails and they fly. They eat worms and crumbs, and sometimes they migrate. It means go to Africa. See when they peck for crumbs they look like they're bowing, like actors at the end of a pantomime. Maybe they're all going to migrate to Mars, so they're bowing to say cheerio. I don't know if birds've got minds, but they must have minds to tell each other it's time to migrate. But they don't look like they've got minds, because they move about in wee jerks like clockwork. Clocks don't have minds. But birds fly, clocks don't. But aeroplanes and spaceships fly and they don't have any minds. Tell you what, put down that you don't know if birds've got minds or not, but put down that the Earthling people *do* have minds in their heads. Now I bet you're wondering what all this has to do with Nature Study. I bet you're saying to yourself, this sounds more like Martian poetry to me. But have you ever thought that the two subjects might be quite the very same? Especially when there's interference on the radio, the two subjects sort of blur with each other, don't they?

I'll tell you something else: my mother put her head in the gas oven and she lost her mind.

Cheerio.

Listen if you don't pay attention, you'll never learn anything. Materialise *this instant*. That's better. If I catch you disappearing again or tuning out, I'm just going to have to make an example of you. Is that clear? Or else I will put you outside the door of your capsule and you will die. You're not stupid, you're lazy. You're a lazy, little *Martian*. You have opened my eyes more than once today and your behaviour is getting deterior-hating. Right, we're going to do some more Martian Nature Study. Any more interference out of you and I will give you long division or even poetry. Put this down:

Nature Study On The Planet Earth.

Under that, put this:

On the Planet Earth, everything is the other way round. Most Earthling birds don't have names and their mothers forget what to call them when they go to visit the nest. The only ones with names are crows, thrushes, blackbirds, sparrows, eagles, vultures and cuckoos. The rest are just called birds. Cuckoos are off their heads, they lay their eggs in the gas oven. My mother can be heard on the first day of Spring, and the noise she makes sounds like her name. She is cuckoo so she lives in a home, her home in another bird's nest. Behaviour means going to Africa, or else abominable long division. A bird is a flying machine, with a screw loose. Cuckoo clocks have minds, as well as hands, faces and speckled breasts. At dawn you can hear them tick, and every tick means deterior-hating. Spring is the time of the year when you scratch your nose for Hello and stick out your tongue for Cheerio. Poetry is people pecking for crumbs without minds in their heads. After a pantomime, the actors migrate. I am dust in the air, I am a reflection. I am the only Earthling with a mind, and the mind is interference from another programme. Koo-koo, koo-koo. Cheerio.

Come in again, do you read me, hello. See that door along there, behind that there's a wee room where you go to get smallpox jags. On the wall there's this chart with letters on it. On the top line the letters are huge, you'd have to be blind not to read them. But they get tinier and tinier as they go down, till you can hardly even see them. See this chart is for testing Earthling eyes. If you don't get far enough down, you get specs. I got specs, but I smashed them on the way to school because everybody was calling me four-eyes.

Nobody's going to call me four-eyes.

The Brains wears specs, but nobody calls her four-eyes. Probably because she's always had specs, so nobody notices them. If you ask me, the Brains was probably *born* with specs on. And I had to get specs because of you. Don't try and deny it. It's with looking at you when you materialise, now my eyes are the wrong way round. I wish I had X-ray eyes, then I could see into all the classrooms, I could see what's happening inside them. The last time I was in that room, that room with the chart on the wall, I got

35

drops in my eyes that made me see a bit like a Martian. People didn't have edges, they sort of merged with each other. Blurred. But once when I was taken into that room, this nurse in a white coat gave me a book to look at. It was a Martian book. Every page was covered all over with hundreds of coloured dots. They looked like they were moving, sort of swarming like wasps. It was like what you see when you look at the sun too long, hundreds of coloured dots moving round. Then this nurse asked me if I could make out the shape or the number. Everybody in the class had to do it, it was a test. I'll tell you this, I was great at it. I was better than anybody else in 4B. If we got tests in making out the shape or the number instead of tests in long division, I'd be getting fucking gold stars every time.

The trouble is we didn't get marks for it. It was to find out if we were colourblind. I'm not colourblind, I *know* the sea's supposed to be blue. It isn't though is it, when you look at it up close? When my mother used to take me to the seaside, the sea always looked more sort of like the colour of piss. And what about the Black Sea, what colour's that? I should ask the teacher: please Miss, is the Black Sea black? Miss, is the Red Sea red? What colour's the Dead Sea, Miss? Is that the one he walked on, or is that the one he parted? Miss how could he part a *sea*? Keep the noise down, it was a miracle. A miracle is something that doesn't happen every day on Earth. On Mars, everything that happens is called a miracle.

She put her head in the Dead Sea. Her mind got walked on, and parted. Keep the noise down, it was a miracle, miracle, miracle.

Over and out.

Hello. See it might be okay getting put outside the door, except everybody sees the patch. That's the deterior thing about it. See everybody knows I've got a patch in the back of my trousers, but when I'm walking out to the door everybody sees it at once. And I can feel this evil thing behind me, like an actor in a pantomime. Maybe people are like birds and don't have minds in their heads, maybe I'm the only Earthling with a mind. Everything else is a pantomime: everything everybody says, everything everybody does. Maybe even the Mad Ringmaster hasn't got a mind. I don't know if he has got a mind, because I can't be him. I've got to be me. But I know I've got a mind, but everything else could be a sort of colourblind pantomime. Like the Brains crying outside but not inside when I broke her fucking coloured pencil and squirted the piss on her specs. And the way my mother used to cry when she was losing her mind. She still does when I go to see her, but it's just like watering eyes. The tears drip out of her eyes like when a tap needs a new washer. She lost her mind, that's why. When you lose your mind on Earth, you go into a home for mental defectors. I've still got a mind, so I'm not going to be going into a home.

Hello mind, take me to Mars.

On Mars, everybody has a mind and you can *see it*. It looks like a page in that colourblind book. You look at all the swarming dots, you don't know what it is, then you make out the shape or the number. And that's what they're thinking, that's the thought. On Earth, people have to use words. They have to talk to each other, or write letters to each other, or phone each other up. If you want to talk to a lot of people at once, you have to be a teacher. Either that or you have to be on the radio or the t.v. Then you can talk to hundreds of people at once. Like the weatherman who was on before that Rhyme Time programme, except there was a lot of interference. Well, he was probably talking to about a million people at once. That's what I'm going to be when I grow up, I'm going to be the weatherman.

Cheerio.

Hello come in are you receiving me. In a few minutes there will be Clock Talk, a programme of verse for cuckoos. Before that we have a weather report from Mars:

This is the Martian weather forecast. Tonight it is going to rain smallpox. The air will be full of interference, and the sea will be going on fire later on. Don't part it or walk on it, and don't go out without getting your jags. Tomorrow morning, the sun is going to be a shape or a number. If you can't make it out, you're colourblind. The clouds are going to start off huge and get tinier and tinier as they go down. If you can't read them, you'll get specs. There will be a lot of abominable behaviour later on, so don't get put outside the door. There will be no gold stars for anybody this week, or the next. Instead the sky is going to be covered in mistakes and blots. In the North, and South, and East, and West, there will be some scattered showers. You're bound to get drops in your eyes. The planet is changing shape. Watch out for meteors. Cheerio.

But if other people don't have minds, there isn't much point in talking to them, is there? Not even to one of them. Maybe you should score out the bit about Earthling people having minds, and put down that some do and some don't. And she doesn't talk to anybody else except herself. See she lost her mind, then went into a home, and now she's got *two minds*. And one mind talks to the other mind, I think. But I wonder if the other mind can hear it. Maybe it's more like interference. But what I can't understand is how one mind take away one mind equals two minds.

Over and out.

Hello this is an SOS. My Oxygen supply is running low and I have made no contact with the *Enterprise*. Beam me up before it's too late.

See down there over that balcony, that's the Assembly Hall. It means prayers. You put your hands together and you say: *Our Father Which Art in Heaven, Hallo'ed Be Thy Name.* Then the Mad Ringmaster stands up and everybody else sits down and listens. He makes a speech about the school. If you've squirted piss on somebody's specs, he reads out your name and you have to report to his study along the corridor there. Or if something's happened in the school, the Mad Ringmaster announces it. Like when one boy died, he announced it so that everybody would know. He said: *Today there is a shadow among us.* He's like you that boy, dematerialised. Nobody can see him. See he fell from a tree, and the blood ran over his brain. His soul went to Heaven, and his mind is a shadow among us. On Mars you probably have a different kind of assembly. You probably just sit in a big circle holding hands, passing messages to each other through your fingertips. Because hundreds of Martians can get together and think *one* thought, because you can sort of merge, can't you? Blur with each other.

I wish I was an alien being. Maybe the next time you materialise, if you touch me we'll maybe merge.

So I had to report to his study. I told everybody about it in the playground, I was the centre of attention. Attention is what you pay for somebody talking to you. It's like buying something with money, you have to pay it to hear what they say. I told them all your name for him, the Mad Ringmaster, but everybody just said his name's Williams. You call him that because that's sort of what he looks like, with his big black gown and curly mustache. And his belt instead of a whip. And I told everybody what he said to me in his study, when he was giving me the belt. You'd better start crying. See, he wanted me to cry on the outside, the way the Brains did, the way my mother does. Like an actor in a pantomime. Then he could make an example of me. He could take me back into the class crying and then I'd be an example.

I am an example. But what am I an example of? I'm an example of *you*, the other way round. I should tell the teacher: Please Miss, I'm the wrong way round. Billy Hope, this is a classroom not a home for mental defectors. Go and stand outside the door. You can come back in when you're the right way round.

But if the Mad Ringmaster ever gets me again, I'm definitely going to go to Mars. He'll have to announce it at assembly: *There is a shadow . . . no not a shadow . . . there is a reflection among us. He got put outside the door, and the blood ran over his brain.* I wish you would exterminate the Mad Ringmaster, make *him* a shadow among us. Put him in a box and bury him, bury him in the Dead Sea. It's wrong to hope somebody dies, except on Mars. What's wrong here on Earth is right on Mars, or at least it's not wrong. Because not wrong isn't the same as right always is it? Like when you get a test, and you don't know some of the answers. So you don't put anything down, you just leave them blank. Well, you're not wrong, are you? But you're not right either, or they'd give you marks. They'd give you a couple of marks for leaving it blank, but they don't, except on Mars.

You know something, if they gave her a test she wouldn't be able to answer any of the questions. She'd got nothing out of a hundred. *Here comes the Mad Ringmaster.*

I'm inside the class again, I can't talk to you. He got me again, for getting put outside the door. He wanted me to cry on the outside again, to make me an example. But I didn't, I cried inside. My hands are on fire, they're Martian's hands. Touch my fingertips, touch. Send messages through my fire. Don't ask me any more questions, blur with me. My hands are full of a thousand stings, so are yours. It feels like a swarm of wasps, a thousand stings. You can feel the message, so can I. It's sore, that's the message. The teacher's reading that poem called Spring from a book. Pay attention, pay attention. Cheerio.

'Billy Hope, stop blowing on your hands. I'm going to read the first verse again, the one you missed because of interference.

39

Perhaps you can tell us what it means, Billy. Listen to the words very carefully:

> *Pretty creatures which people the sky*
> *Are thousandfold this day,*
> *Feathered choristers, they that sing*
> *The livelong day away.*

Now, Billy, I want you . . .'

I am an alien being and I people the thousandfold sky.

'I want *you* to tell the class . . . what the feathered choristers are.'

My Mother put her head in the sky and her mind flew away.

'Birds.'

The Full Moon

'WHAT IS IT?' asked the American lady. Unwittingly, she had voiced my thoughts — I was looking at her extravagant hairstyle and thinking exactly that: what *is* it? It looked like esparto grass trying to look like ice cream. But the enigma she was talking about was something of mine — a decoration I'd been making for the Halloween party in Ward One. I'd become so engrossed in the simple pleasure of making something that I'd scarcely noticed the visiting party. Besides, I had been working in the Therapy Unit for over a year and I'd come to regard the many visiting parties as something of an annoyance. I tended to ignore these processions of cheerful strangers — at times they made me think of sight-seeing tourists — and get on with what I was doing while the psychiatrists showed them round. The Halloween decoration had been coming along nicely: I'd cut out a large disc shape from a sheet of card. One side I'd painted black, the other I'd adorned with golden paper, cut to size. To the bright side I'd added, with glue and glitter, the image of a smiling face. Then I'd attached a long line of thread, so that it could be suspended from the ceiling in Ward One.

'It's the full moon, ' I said.

She picked up the moon by its thread, then held it out at arm's length the better to appreciate it — and avoid the glue.

'My, it's gorgeous,' she said.

This was praise, but it was praise from a woman with a frightening hairstyle, wearing a lime-green twin-set. Pinned to her lapel there was a rectangular identity badge, and under the name I made out words which told me that she had come from the Psychology Department of an illegible university. She turned to one of her colleagues, a young man in a brown velvet suit, also sporting a badge.

'Ain't it cute?' she said to him. In the vicinity of his nose there grew a sparse mustache, which resembled the dirty marks often left by elastoplasts. His vague brown eyes tried to focus on my

41

makeshift planet. Dangling from Twin-set's finger on its thread, it revolved of its own accord . . . now the dark side, now the bright.

'Yeah,' he said, 'what is it?' From the tone of his voice it was clear that he had been looking at people and their little achievements all day.

'It's the *moon*!' cooed Twin-set. She gave me a slow, sly wink which made me think of a television programme I had once seen, to do with the habits of lizards.

'Mmm,' said Mustache, 'quite a moon. You gonna put that gold stuff on this side too?' He was pointing to the side I'd painted black. My moon did a quick about-turn, as if to invalidate the question.

'That's the dark side,' I said. Twin-set gave out a short squeak of delight.

'Did you hear that?' she whispered excitedly. 'He says that's the *dark* side — ain't that adorable?'

I noticed that my status had changed, somewhere along the line, from the second to the third person singular. She gave me a benign smile, and as she laid my cardboard satellite on the table, she enunciated her praise volubly, as if she thought I might be deaf:

'It's a bee-oo-tiful moon!' she said.

I was beginning to wonder why so much was being made of what was, after all, only a decoration, when I felt the lady's hand gently patting the crown of my head. I felt a curious tingling all over my scalp, which then ran down the back of my neck and swarmed up and down my spine — a sensation I would normally associate with moments of acute embarrassment, anger, pleasure, or seeing ghosts. I was forced to realise it: *they thought I was one of the patients.*

It was the first time I had been taken for a *bona-fide* mental defective, and for an instant I caught a glimpse of what it was to be treated as such and I panicked. I stood up abruptly, causing the chair I'd been sitting on to crash to the floor behind me. Immediately, Johnny threw his paintbrush to the floor and ran out of the room, slamming the door as he went. Johnny was a patient with many eccentricities, personality disorders, ontological anxieties or call them what you will, and sometimes he would take a loud noise or a sudden movement to be an insult, directly aimed at his person. It had happened many times before, and I knew that he would run back to Ward One, then the nurses would calm him down and send him back to Therapy.

Mustache and Twin-set exchanged a meaningful glance, then I felt a hand on my shoulder.

'Sit down,' said Mustache, 'it's all right.' He righted my chair and pushed it into the backs of my legs. I looked around for another member of staff, but they had all gone into the Crafts Department with the other members of the visiting party.

'He's a bit jumpy,' said Twin-set, 'I think we should leave him alone.'

'We gotta be getting *along*,' said Mustache, unsure of how much of the message was getting through to me.

I raised my hand to detain them. I needed to explain. It was easy. All I had to say was: 'Actually, I'm not a patient at all; I'm a member of staff.' I might add, just for good measure, that I was in reality a Philosophy Graduate, working here in the Therapy Unit as a preventative expedient against unemployment. In my confusion I was able to utter three words. All three were mono-syllabic, and I said them without much conviction:

'I . . . work . . . here,' I said.

'Sure you do,' said Mustache, 'siddown.'

'You should do some more work on that moon,' said Twin-set, 'I don't think it should have a dark side.'

She picked up the full moon and turned it over, so that it lay with the dark side up. Unaccountably, I did nothing to demonstrate my status as a sane, rational *employee*, but chose instead to reverse her action. I turned the moon over again, so that it lay with the bright side up. In its smiling golden face I saw my own features loom and distort.

'I figure he wants to keep one side of it black,' said Mustache.

I looked at his face, then Twin-set's, then his again. Both wore placatory smiles, but in their eyes I could read the vexation. It was as if I were a creature of a different species, one which might inhabit the dark side of the moon. I could not help myself — in a spasm of silent laughter, I sank weakly into the seat. I went on shuddering with laughter while, behind my back, they discussed me: what did I *have*? They spoke of Autism, Paranoia, Chronic Schizophrenia for all the world as if these were ailments people *had*, like measles! I wanted to correct them, I wanted to suggest that these were modes of being, that schizophrenia is something a person *is* . . . but I was giggling like a maniac and, after all, irrational laughter could be the symptom of anything. But now my IQ was the moot point: was I low-grade, or high-grade?

'I don't know,' whispered Twin-set, 'but I'd sure like to look at his case-notes. Did you see the way he looked at us just then? He's weird.' My diagnosis had come: weird. A terminal case of weirdness.

'Mmm,' said Mustache, 'it makes you wonder what's going on inside his head. You know, I'm sure some of these people are in touch with things which are uh . . . inaccessible to us, except maybe in dreams . . .'

As my fit of laughter subsided, I noticed that Billy, sitting at the far end of the room, was sniggering into his hand. All the other patients — apart from Johnny, of course — had continued with their work in an orderly, methodical way, but Billy had been observing the whole episode and now he was sniggering conspic-uously. The sight made me shudder slightly, because Billy had forgotten how to snigger — he was a patient who seldom spoke, or did anything at all of his own volition. He waited until he was told what to do, then he made his gesture of obedience. His apathy was almost impenetrable: he slouched in his seat, appeared to stare into space for hours, and often his mouth hung open. He looked always disconsolate, bored. I watched with growing fascination as he made some pretence of looking at his drawing, while his features contorted into this unaccustomed thing which looked like pain but wasn't. It was laughter. I had known him for over a year and it was the first time I had seen him laugh.

'That moon's amazing,' said Twin-set to Mustache. They were making for the door into the Crafts Department. 'You know that old wives' tale about how the full moon affects them?'

'Oh sure, I've heard about that.' Mustache gave a little laugh.

'Well, you wouldn't *believe* what one of the nurses in the wards was telling me today . . .'

They waved their little bye-byes to me and closed the door behind them. My sanity was restored. On Billy's face there lingered an unmistakable smirk. Then less than a smirk, then nothing. I watched as his lower lip sagged, until his mouth hung open. He resumed his drawing, but his pencil scarcely touched the paper.

When I rang up Ward One, a nurse told me that Johnny had arrived in an agitated state.

'He said something about the full moon,' she said, 'but it isn't full just now, is it?'

'No, I'd been *making* a moon, out of card, and gold paper . . . It's a decoration, you see, for the Halloween party in your ward.'

She made a small, non-commital noise.

'It's difficult to explain what happened,' I said. 'Is Johnny ready to come back over yet?'

'Oh, he's all right now. Mind you, some people say it does affect them.'

I mumbled something ungrammatical about people fearing madness more than death, then told her to send Johnny back to Therapy when he was ready.

I sat down at the table where I had been working. I turned the moon over and looked at the side I'd painted black. Perhaps it shouldn't have a dark side? I picked it up by its thread and held it out at arm's length. It turned, slowly . . . now the bright side, now the dark. Billy looked up from his drawing, but his pencil went on whispering against the paper.

'Hey Billy,' I said, 'ain't it cute?'

'Yeah,' he said quietly, 'what is it?'

Norman and the Man

NORMAN IS drawing a circle, and the man is watching him. It's a big circle, it wants to involve the whole page. Ominous, thinks the man. The way they grow, spreading like circles in water. Norman's mind is dark, wide water — who knows what's living in there? Standing over Norman, watching the line coil slowly around to meet itself, the man is mesmerised. It's as if, in a hopeless gesture, the man has thrown an idea into the darkness. And now he can stand back and watch, watch the disturbance it makes: one by one, and with a great deal of care, he makes circle after circle. It has become Norman's work, his calling. They are only circles, thinks the man. Or not-quite-circles: each one is a little different.

The man has another idea. He goes away and comes back with a small round mirror. He gives the mirror to Norman. Norman grips it with both hands, looks at it. He reacts as a dog or a cat might react on seeing its own reflection: curious for a moment, troubled perhaps, then bored. But unlike a dog or a cat, Norman throws the mirror to the floor. By the time the man has picked up all the pieces, Norman has forgotten all about the mirror — he's getting his circle to touch, his empty circle. What was the man hoping for, some sign of recognition? It could be that at last, when he's done so many circles, Norman will look into one of them and recognise something there: himself, his own reflection. In the meantime it's hard work for Norman, getting that line to bend, getting the circle to touch. Soon the man won't have a size of paper to contain it, this voluminous shape of Norman's. Then the man may have another idea: give Norman a piece of chalk, let him chalk his circle on the floor. Or outside, around the Therapy Unit, around the hospital and all its grounds, then around the city, the country . . . Ominous, thinks the man. Norman's circle could surround the world. Then everyone would have to live and die inside Norman's circle . . . but he's torn the paper again.

Start again, Norman, again. Hard work, making the circle. Let's do it one more time. Tea-time soon, biscuit.

And with sticky-tape the man fixes a clean sheet of paper to the table, so that this time it won't be torn. And with one hand flat on the table, and with his face an inch from the page, Norman begins again: time after time, it's endless. The man walks around the room, looking at the pictures being done by all the others. All the others like Norman, but not quite: each case is a little different, as is each picture: that landscape with its mammoth black sun; the vermilion christ on his cross; dark, unnamable beasts grazing in a violet pasture; one small Matisse of unlikely flowers; a self-portrait with lidless eyes. Everyone is doing a picture except the man. The man is the only one who can stand back and watch. Perhaps at one time the man could do pictures too, but now it seems that he can't. And perhaps that is why he is here: to show the others how to do what he can no longer do. He sits on a desk by the window, looking out at the hospital grounds: mosaic of yellows, reds and browns. Winter soon, thinks the man, then Spring.

Start again, Norman, again. We want to get here, here. Here's where the circle begins, and here's where it ends. No short cuts, or it won't be a circle. A circle, Norman, a circle. Or else the moon won't be full.

Now the man is reading a report, a report about Norman. It says that he is twenty-five, mental age questionmark. It says that he was admitted on a certain day more then twenty-four years ago. It says brain damage, severe motor difficulties. It says physiotherapy recommended, protective clothing and footwear. When he puts away the report, the man looks at Norman's clothes: a leather headguard, like a boxer's; elasticated trousers, grey; shoes with thick, wide soles which turn up at the toes. Walking is hard work for Norman, and very often he fails. Every step, thinks the man, must be deliberated. And for every action the effort must be grotesque. Norman's movements, thinks the man, so laboured, so wooden . . . they are more like guesses at motion. As if he is somewhere far above his body, too far above that crude puppet to know with any certainty which wire moves which jointed limb. Norman must jerk the wire and hope that the head will nod, that the hand is raised, that the foot will find the floor. That those dangling hands will parody a human gesture. Every day he walks from his ward to here, the place where he makes his circles. The man helps him off with his coat, because Norman can't do buttons.

At last, Norman has finished: his slow, slow circle is complete. Now he'll get his tea in the blue plastic cup with the lid — it's the kind of cup infants use. It's his, he knows it's his.

Tea-time Norman, biscuit. Hard work, Norman, hard work. Now, look at the circle: it's the moon, Norman, the moon. Is it good?

Norman opens his mouth and utters: AAAH!

It means yes, it is good. The circle has a certain AAAH. And when Norman has finished his tea, and when Norman has eaten his biscuit, he lets the cup fall to the floor and he rests: head down, his cheek on the table, one arm dangling loose by his side, with his legs splayed apart, with his twisted feet . . . Like a puppet, thinks the man, when the man who pulls the wires is away.

Tomorrow a clean sheet of paper, and another circle by Norman. Does he get bored with it, day after day, making circle after circle? Yes, he gets bored, and the man gets bored: wishing the day were done, the season over, the year. Winter soon, then Spring.

He can stand at the window and watch it: like a brief, accidental mark on a blank page, there is a tiny figure against the snow. It moves, it grows. Such excruciating progress it makes, the man wonders why it doesn't give up. He sees it falling and getting up again, resuming the pilgrimage. The gait is like a metronome, thinks the man, head swerving wildly to right and to left. When he loses the rhythm he falls, then the page looks blank. Perhaps this time he'll stay down, but no.

The snow on the path has been compressed by many feet, and even the man must tread carefully. When Norman sees the man he stops, one foot in the air, and raises a hand to greet him. The foot comes down missing the ground, and Norman throws both arms up in consternation. He falls, it is the only thing he does quickly, flat on his back. The man covers his mouth with his hand, laughing because he can't help laughing, as at a fallen clown. And even as he approaches, even as he extends his hand to him and hears his animal cry of outrage, and even when he sees that the clown's mouth is not a smile after all but a deep stripe of despair, even then the man can't *help* . . . But everything is reversed and it is the man who bellows his outrage, the man who is being laughed at, the man who has slipped and fallen on his back, and now who is the clown with the mouth of despair? And after a moment Norman and the man are both laughing at each other. If someone were to pass by now, what would they see but two grown men sitting down in the snow, laughing at each other?

Okay Norman, it was the moon but today it's going to be the sun. No sun in the sky, Norman, until you put one there. Today, a clean sheet of paper.

But as the man tries to help him to his feet, Norman resists. He shakes his head from side to side. He doesn't want to get up, apparently. Apparently he wants to sit there in the snow. Then, reaching out as if to retrieve something he has lost, Norman begins to dig up the snow with the fingers of one hand. Where he furrows it up, the black of the path begins to show through.

Get up, Norman, get up.

But now the black begins to grow into a line, and the line begins to bend and yes, it is indisputable: with his hand he is digging a circle. The man joins in, digging up the snow on his side, disclosing a black arc. And soon they will touch, making a circle to end all circles — it's bound to surround them both. And if someone were to pass by now, what would they see?

Walking up the slippery path, it's like two drunk men going home: hard to say who is taking whom. Both swerve, stagger, collide. When they are inside, the man begins to help Norman off with his coat, but Norman wants to play his little game with the man: he grabs the man's arm and holds on to it tightly, gets his other hand around his neck and pulls him forward. When they are face to face, Norman looks into the man's eyes — who knows what's living in there?

Let go, Norman, let go.

But he has a vice-like grip, and will let the man go when he pleases. That's the little game Norman plays with the man, but the man doesn't like the little game of looking into each other's eyes. And when he is free the man makes Norman work again: gets his paper taped to the table, his paint brush in his hand, his chair pushed in and he's ready. Norman gets into the mood, gets a grip of the situation, his mind into gear, then:

The sun, Norman, the sun. Without it, no light, none. Everything dark, cold.

Holding the brush as if it were a dagger, Norman makes a slow stab at the water-pot, then grinds the brush into the paint. He begins the thick black outline, and later he'll fill it in. The man stands back, watching: what moves upon the face of the waters? What light from a black, black sun?

Does he see that they are good? Sun, moon, planets: it's Norman's universe. Now he goes through his portfolio, examining each, one by one. It takes an age to look at them, to review and appreciate each. Every so often Norman grabs the man's arm and shows him one, pointing a finger at its empty centre.

Norman opens his mouth and utters: AAAH!

Let go, Norman, let go.

The man collects together Norman's circles and puts them away in a drawer, because now he has another idea. He gets a clean sheet of paper, sits down beside Norman, signals to him to pay attention. Norman yawns, looks bored. The man takes a pencil and begins, with a great deal of care, to draw:

A circle, Norman, a circle.

Norman nods his head, yawns. A circle, of course it is, what else could it be. Then, inside the circle, the man draws another circle. It is much smaller than the first. Next to it, another small circle. Norman laughs, yawns. It doesn't take the man long to make a circle touch.

Two little circles inside a big circle. Eyes, Norman, eyes.

The man touches the circles, then points to his eyes. He makes a circle with his finger and thumb and holds it in front of his eye. Then he adds to the drawing:

And this is the nose, and the mouth.

And to the head is added a body, to the body arms and legs. Circles for hands and feet, circles for the buttons of his coat. It's simple, it's rudimentary.

A man, Norman, a man. It's you, Norman, look:

The man points to the drawing of the man, then points to Norman. Norman looks at the drawing. Curious for a moment, troubled perhaps, then he shakes his head from side to side and throws the pencil to the floor. He grabs the man's arm, wants to play his little game, but the man doesn't want to play. He pushes Norman away, then repeats the process: two small circles inside of a big one. Nose, mouth, ears. And to the head a body, to the body arms and legs. He hands the pencil to Norman, and Norman throws it to the floor. Norman rests his cheek on the table, lets his arms dangle down by his sides. The man stands up, walks around the room looking at the pictures: a smiling face with the legend 'GOOD BOY' written above it; a thickly crayoned dinosaur confronts the words 'THE STONEAGE'; inside a dark tunnel, a figure carrying a torch; the tree with its green, mysterious fruit; tiny, swastikad aeroplanes, on fire in a rain of bullets. The man sits down by the window, looks out at the sunlight, the trees. There is a faint green haze around the branches, and the buds are beginning to appear. The effort begins again, the colossal effort of things. The man looks at Norman's face and sees an empty circle.

Everyone is sitting out in the garden. The tables and the chairs have been brought outside, and now everyone is sitting in the sunshine drawing or painting a picture. Everyone except Norman and the man. Norman is oblivious to the heat, the insects, the birdsong, because he has fallen asleep: his head has drooped on to the table, covering the drawing he's done. His hands are dangling down by the sides of his wheelchair and his pencil is lying in the grass nearby. The man is indoors, writing a report on Norman. It says that Norman has a broken ankle and will require a wheelchair until he is able to walk again.

The man comes out into the garden and walks around looking at the pictures. When he comes to Norman, he shakes him by the shoulder.

And slowly he comes to life: the hand fumbles at his eyes, his nose and his mouth, as if he's trying to pluck the sleep from his face. Norman sits up slowly, moving like a man underwater. He screws up his eyes, looks up at the sun. He opens his mouth and utters: AAAH!

The man retrieves the pencil from the grass. Norman laughs, startled. It's a trick the man has done, a conjuring trick. Everything is a conjuring trick. The man offers Norman his pencil, but he shakes his head from side to side and yawns. He doesn't want to draw, apparently. He's finished his drawing. The man looks at it: a mess of heavy black lines and circles. It makes the man look away.

What is it, Norman, what is it?

Norman laughs, nods his head slowly, stabs at the picture with his finger. The man sees a muddle of misshapen curves, overlapping and smudged hopelessly. Curious for a moment, troubled perhaps, then he looks away. Norman grabs at the man's arm, gets his other hand behind his neck, pulls him down until they're face to face. The man sees a tiny version of himself in the pupil of Norman's eye.

Let go, Norman, let go!

The man loosens Norman's fingers from his neck and pulls away. He goes indoors, to his reports.

Norman looks at the drawing on the table in front of him. It's his, he knows it's his. He points to a tangle of circles, then slowly lifts a hand to his eyes. He stabs with his finger at the heavy scribble above, then claps a hand on his headguard. He goes on, although the man is no longer beside him, pointing to the drawing, then pointing to a part of himself. To those buttons all sizes and shapes, to the multitude of twisted arms and hands. To the feet more monstrous than the face, to the wheels overlapping the legs. He opens his mouth to utter, but the man can't hear. And at last it is Norman who must wait for the man. It could be that at last, when he has looked at so many of the drawings, the man will look into one of them and recognise something there: that although it is laboured and grotesque, and although it makes him want to look away, it is the image of a man nonetheless and he is recognisable.

From the Diary of Billy Bible

MONDAY

Today I am in Therapy again it being Monday. I am in Therapy five days a week now because I am good. On Saturday and Sunday I am in the ward because Therapy is shut. There is nothing to do in the ward so I do nothing except what the nurses tell me. If I had a friend like Peter in the ward it would be better but I have no friend like Peter in the ward. In Therapy I do pictures mostly of Christ Our Saviour on the cross. Mister Cuthbert calls them crucifixions. I did so many Mister Cuthbert had to put them in the store room. Then he said I was to stop doing those crucifixions and do something else. Then I started doing the tunnels. Mister Cuthbert said they all look the same but when I do one I remember something different from the last one. Mister Cuthbert says I am a born artist. I think I will do another tunnel today.

TUESDAY

I have been reading the Bible my father sent me a long time ago being a minister of God. He sent me the Bible and a letter and a steel clip to stop wet dreams. It was just after I came here. I started putting the steel clip on like I did at home before I went to bed at night. Because I am good I am good. But I showed it to one of the male nurses and asked him to guess what it was for like I asked my friend Peter a long time ago. The male nurse took it away from me when he found out what it was for and ever since then it has been hard to be good. But I still have the Bible and I always take it with me everywhere in my jacket pocket. Once I lost it but I got it back again. It has my name on the page before Genesis. The part I like to read most is the Creation. I am always reading it so the nurses call me Billy Bible. It says the earth was without form and void and darkness was upon the face of the deep. Peter is like that now without form and void now that he is dead. I think I will do another tunnel today.

Mister Cuthbert says if I do more tunnels he will have to put them in the store room with the crucifixions. I don't like the pictures I do being put in the store room. When I want to look at them I have to get a key from Mister Cuthbert. I don't like going into the store room because of the darkness upon the face of the deep and the rats. Mister Cuthbert tried to kill the rats with cobalt blue poison but they ate the poison and got stronger. They eat anything the rats. They eat the wool and the paper in the store room and the foam rubber the sewing women put inside the soft toys they make. Sometimes you are in the bathroom and when you go to wash your hands you see their teethmarks in the bar of soap. It is light in the bathroom but in the store room there are no windows. When you switch on the light in there it takes a little while to come on. It is called a strip light that light in the store room. I don't like being in the store room with the darkness and the rats before the light comes on. I don't like the no windows darkness you get in the store room and some other places for instance the ward. The ward has great big windows but you still get the no windows darkness when you wake up in the middle of the night after a wet dream. Then it is all around you everywhere all over the face of the deep. Then you see a torch coming down between the beds and the night nurses come and say keep it quiet. I takes me a while to know it is the night nurses. I am talking to my friend Peter then I hear them saying to me it's all right Billy the train isn't coming tonight. They don't know it already has.

The tunnel has no windows. It is deep and dark in there and I am running out of black.

WEDNESDAY

Today I was taken out for an outing because I am good. Mister Cuthbert took me and four others in Therapy to an art gallery. In the art gallery Mister Cuthbert showed me a picture with three parts called a TRIPTYCH. This is what the TRIPTYCH was like. In the middle part it was Christ Our Saviour on the cross like some of mine but with details. Mister Cuthbert showed me all the details for instance the hair and the crown of thorns and the blood just above the eye. In the side parts there were a lot of little soldiers and a lot of little women all crying. On the way back to the mini-bus I saw a butcher's shop. There were dead beasts without heads hanging from steel hooks on a big steel rail.

This afternoon I did Christ Our Saviour on the cross with details for instance the hair and the steel hooks and the blood above the eye. Mister Cuthbert put it up but he took it down again because it made one of the sewing women scream out loud and throw her felt-work snake on the floor. Mister Cuthbert took it down again and put it in the store room with the others. I am worried because if the rats eat Christ Our Saviour on the cross they will get stronger than people. I saw one today it was big and brown like burnt sienna with a long tail. It ran along the wall in Therapy and I think it went into the store room.

Tomorrow I think I will do a TRIPTYCH with three parts. In the middle tunnel I will do the inside of a church with the minister of God reading the Bible. In the side parts the night nurses coming down between the rails and me and my friend Peter all crying.

THURSDAY

Today Mister Cuthbert brought a mirror into Therapy. It was lying on a table in the pottery room when I came in. When I looked at it I saw my head dark with the light on the ceiling behind it. Mister Cuthbert says it is his mirror from his home. It has three parts like a TRIPTYCH. He brought it over to my table and he said do a self portrait Billy. He put it on my table against the wall and it is still there. He took away the three tunnels and he brought me a clean sheet of paper. I said I have never done a self portrait of anyone before so he showed me all the details in the mirror.

I don't look the same as before. I have not looked in a mirror for a long time and now I look different. I am still neat and tidy. I put water on my hair before I comb it and I wash myself every night and every morning and I fold my clothes because I am good. But now my shirt is torn at the collar and my jacket is dirty. One leg of my glasses is held on with a piece of elastoplast and now they don't sit right on my nose. My eyes are staring and dark like the cover of the Bible and my face has no details for instance the hair. The head has no blood no crown of thorns and my face is without form and void.

I think I will do a self portrait with three parts like a TRIPTYCH. In the side parts a lot of little sewing women making soft toys and a lot of little Mister Cuthberts all crying.

FRIDAY

Mister Cuthbert said to finish the self portrait but I am doing a tunnel. I did the eyes the hair and the mouth the ears then I saw it was my friend Peter not me in the mirror. I told Mister Cuthbert but he said it looked quite like me and to finish it. So I started the tunnel on top of it. You can still see Peter's face in the tunnel it is the face of the deep. I can't remember anything before the tunnel but when I do one I remember something more. This time I remembered something more about the tunnel and the steel clip to stop wet dreams.

It is harder to be good now without the steel clip before you go to bed and you wake up in the middle of your sleep. The steel clip had little teeth that cut into you where you were dreaming the wet dream and it woke you up before the train came. But our suffering is nothing to the suffering of Christ Our Saviour on the cross.

One of the male nurses took it away when I asked him to guess like Peter and I have never seen it again.

I wasn't supposed to go where the tunnel was my father said not to go there being a minister of God.

Peter did not want to go through the tunnel because of the darkness and the rats. Then I showed him the steel clip and I said guess what it is for. I told my friend Peter I would tell him about the steel clip and what it was for if he came through the tunnel. I liked my friend Peter because he was scared of my father.

I was bad in the tunnel when the train came I pushed my friend Peter into the deep and now that is where he is.

I am in hospital to make me good again. Christ Our Saviour is with me on the cross in the store room with the darkness and the rats. Peter is with me in the tunnel where I put his face instead of the mirror.

Mister Cuthbert came over to see the self portrait and when he saw it he shook his head.

MONDAY

Today I am in Therapy again it being Monday. Last night I had a dream and I woke up in the middle of the tunnel. I saw a torch far away and I thought it was the men coming for Peter. It was the night nurses coming down between the beds to tell me to keep it quiet. They said it's all right Billy the train isn't coming tonight. They don't know it already has.

I have been reading the Bible my father sent me a long time ago. And a letter and a steel clip to guess what it is for. I have still got the letter in my inside jacket pocket but I spilled the paint water on it and the words ran. It said be good and keep yourself neat and tidy Billy do what the the nurses tell you Christ Our Saviour will help you read the Bible and put the steel clip on before you go to bed.

The letter is all yellow now like a piece of skin and I can't read it. I was reading the part about the Creation so the nurses call me Billy Bible. It said the earth was without form and void and darkness was upon the face of the deep. I always stop reading when I get to the deep.

Mister Cuthbert says I am a born artist. I think I will do another tunnel today.

Killing Time

ARCHIE NEWTON held his feet out to the sides and watched the pedals go round on their own: round and round dementedly, because of the fixed wheel. That was the only thing he didn't like about the bike — that, and the dynamo he couldn't get going. His dad would've fixed it in a flash. The man was a genius when it came to bicycle repairs. Handy with clocks he was too, got them going again in no time. Archie had got the bike when he'd died, and his watch, and the old-fashioned lighter with the flip-open lid. The watch had stopped working already — stuck just before noon, or midnight — and now the dynamo . . . but he wouldn't need lights until the winter. By that time he might have a job, he might have a *motorbike*.

'Wrrrummm, *wrrrumm!*' said Archie, the way he had done when he was younger.

He waited till it slowed down, slipped his feet back on to the pedals, then started going as hard as he could. When he got to the path between the swingpark and the bowling green, he held his feet out to the sides again and closed his eyes and waited for the Feeling. He had discovered the Feeling years ago, during the summer holidays between primary and secondary school. And he still got the Feeling when he rode fast enough over the ridged concrete of the path. The bike shook so violently that he could feel the shudders coming up through his body, till his head began to feel fuzzy and . . . and then he fell off, unless he opened his eyes in time.

It was worth falling off for the Feeling.

He picked up the bike and cursed. Two kids who were playing on the merry-go-round jumped off and jeered at him. They doubled up, held their sides and cried *Oh-ho-ho, ee-hee-hee* in a parody of laughter. Archie spat at them, a dry little spit of contempt, but they went on jeering. He watched their antics and frowned.

There was something serious in their ridicule, something joyless. He turned away and surveyed the bike for damage. The chain had come off again.

'Bastard,' said Archie to the bike.

The strident voices behind his back redoubled their laughter. A forced, false laughter, but contagious for all that. Suddenly he couldn't help joining in with it. After a few minutes of trying to keep it in, he sat down on the path beside the bike and let it out. There was triumph in ridicule, but in madness there was release: his body rocked back and forwards until at last it lay on the warm concrete, twitching with laughter. When he stood up again he saw that the kids had stopped. They stared at him in silence, horrified, *appalled*.

'What are you lookin at ya bastartn fuckin wee shites?' said Archie. 'Fuck off or Ah'll come owre there an gie yez a punch in the mooth!'

He heard his own voice going on like that, heaping threat on threat, curse on curse. It was his voice all right, but it didn't sound like his own. It sounded more like his dad's. He'd caught himself doing things too, just the way he moved a hand or found himself sitting in a chair, that reminded him of the old man.

He put the chain back on, then wiped his fingers on the knees of his jeans — already black with oily smears. He looked through the bowling green railings to where a sprinkler was spinning a fine whirl of spray. On the other side of it, some old men were laying out the rubber mats and practising their throws — about to start their game. Archie noticed that among them there was a young girl — she couldn't be much older than him. She was walking to the far end of the green, carrying the jack in her hand. He shaded his eyes with a hand, like a red indian, the way he had done when he was younger. She had long brown hair and from here she looked . . . okay. He could see no sign of Starky, the greenkeeper. He'd probably be in the pavilion, not listening to his transistor. Starky always did that when he had nothing to do. Sat there not hearing the music, staring out at the green. Once, Archie had asked him why he never switched it off, and Starky had said that it made the time go quicker. That was like something his dad had sometimes said about work: when you're busy, the time goes quicker. But time was Time, wasn't it? So how could it go quicker?

Archie looked at the watch his dad had worn and smiled. The time was the same as always: a minute to twelve. The watch didn't work but he still wore it because, well, it was still a watch.

He ran over to the roundabout, grabbed hold of the iron handrails and started to make it go. The kids jumped clear, screeching and yelling in a mockery of panic and outrage. They stood back and watched as he made the wooden hexagon spin. He put one foot up on the footboard and pounded the concrete with the other, till he could feel the centrifugal push and had to tighten his grip. When it was going round and round dementedly he brought his other foot up.

He bent over the seat and peered through the wooden slats at what was underneath: a kaleidoscope of whirring litter and dirt, with long stripes of light where the sun came through the slats. He tried to read some of the names on the sweetwrappers as the light swung over them: *Milk Choc-* . . . *Tobler-* . . . *smrts* . . . *Wag wheeee-*

When he looked up again he saw the kids flash past. Swings, the pavilion, blur of railings, bike, more railings, concrete, the kids. The two of them stood side by side, engrossed in this spectacle of endless motion . . . round and round. He scudded the heel of his gymshoe on the concrete to slow down, then bent over the seat and peered again between the slats, moving the roundabout round a little at a time. Once he'd seen a fifty pence piece underneath. Charlie had lay down on his back and stretched his arm in beneath the footboard, while Archie had held the roundabout still and given him directions from above: 'Left a bit, along a bit, back . . .' It would be harder to get the money out on his own, and anyway he couldn't see any. Just old lollipop sticks, sweetwrappers and dirt.

He staggered a little when he jumped off the roundabout, so the kids started holding their sides again and doing their pantomime of laughter. Strange the way they weren't really amused, but went through these motions like actors rehearsing a scene. Everything was a bit like that in the park, like a piece of make-believe. The painted wooden pavilion, like a stage prop from a western. Starky the parky, trying to make the time go quicker. The shaved and levelled lawn of the green . . . it didn't look like grass. And the people strolling up and down the paths, and these kids.

Archie made to kick them and they made as if to run away. Then he did kick one of them and he squealed with real fright. The other one shouted:

'We'll tell oan you, ya big bastard, you're too big tae play oan the swings!'

Archie felt the voice rising up inside him again, but stopped it before it started.

'Nyaa,' he said, turning away.

As soon as his back was turned the kid who'd been kicked stopped squealing. It hadn't been much of a kick anyway, more of a soft thump on the behind, but from it Archie had taken some small satisfaction. It had worked too, because now the kids went back to the roundabout and let him be.

He walked to the chute and hoisted himself up in big strides, taking six or seven of the tiny steps at a time. At the top there was a kind of cage of iron bars. He climbed up on top of the cage and dangled his feet over the sides, the way he had done when he was younger. He took out the cigarette he'd pinched from his mum's packet and put it between his lips. He lit up, closed the lighter and turned it over in his palm. Somehow he knew that when the wick or the flint ran out, or when it ran out of petrol, he wouldn't do anything about it. He'd just let it stop working, like the watch and the dynamo. Everything was going that way anyway, winding down, running out of whatever kept it going. It was the way things wanted to go.

He looked over the park to where he lived, but couldn't tell which house was his, or even which street. He knew it was empty anyway. His mum would still be at work, the kids at school. Since his dad had died, everything in the house had been breaking down. The lights in the hall and the upstairs landing had stopped working, fused. It was up to him to fix them, but he'd always found an excuse. It had happened gradually, but it had happened — everybody had stopped bothering. Even about getting a job, making a start in life and all that, Archie had not only stopped caring but had stopped pretending to care. When his mum made some suggestion now — her latest idea was night school — he just shrugged and got on with what he was doing. What he was doing was usually nothing.

Beyond the brown roofs he could see the Forth, and the fire-topped chimneys of Grangemouth. Charlie was somewhere over there right now, playing with one of the biggest chemistry sets in the world. Hard to believe that Charlie, mad Charlie who'd do absolutely anything for a laugh, who'd done no more work than Archie had at school, had found a job in a *laboratory*. How was it possible? Archie tried to imagine him at work, wearing a white lab-coat and a collar and tie, arranging the test-tubes in long wooden racks, labelling pyrex beakers full of strangely coloured liquids, writing down the enigmatic formulae. And going to the canteen for his lunch, and sitting at a table with *scientists*. And all the other experts: chemists, engineers, computer people, time and motion men . . . and Charlie! How could it be?

Archie looked over the bowling green and noticed that Starky had come out of the pavilion and was fiddling with the sprinkler. He'd turned the water off, and now he was moving it to another part of the green. It was strange to watch him at his slow labour, oblivious of everything except his little task: to move it from here to there, then from there to somewhere else. That was work, it was what Starky had to do. He had to do it because he was the greenkeeper and the green had to be kept green. That was what all work was like: keeping the green green green. Because when they couldn't work any more, the old men needed to play. But they couldn't remember how to, so they needed a game to play at, a game with rules and scorecards and balls of wood and a nice green green with a pavilion to put on their overshoes in, so as not to mark the green. And that was why Starky was so engrossed in moving the sprinkler, because he was the greenkeeper keeping the green.

Archie watched Starky marching back into the pavilion, and a moment later the water was spinning from the sprinkler again. Charlie had always made fun of Starky, imitating his slow gestures and his doleful, let's-take-one-thing-at-a-time way of talking. One night they'd sprayed their nicknames, Chic and Titch, on the back wall of the pavilion:

'Ah wish Ah could see his face when he sees it!'

'He prob'ly wilnae even notice it —'

'He's *bound* tae see it. Imagine what he'll say!'

'He'll say . . . he'll say: What. Have. They. Buggers. Done tae ma PAVILION!'

Archie smiled at the memory of it, but without Charlie it

wasn't so much fun hanging round in the park. Charlie was moving on to other things — learning to drive, getting a girlfriend. Archie was still riding around on his bike, and he'd even got into the habit of calling in on *Starky* just to pass the time.

The two kids had come over to the chute, and one of them was already half-way up the steps.

'We'll tell oan you,' he shouted, 'you're too *wee* tae smoke!'

Archie flicked the smouldering end in his direction and watched it do a tiny somersault through the air. The kids made faces and blew raspberries. Instead of going down the chute, Archie caught hold of the support poles and swung down between them. Something made him hang there as long as he could, dangling between the poles and being jeered at by the kids, his feet some two yards above the ground. He saw his tall shadow on the concrete and closed his eyes and waited for the Pain.

From the pavilion came the hysterical sound of an accordion playing a reel. He leaned the bike up against the wooden balustrade and looked at the dancing spray of water. Round and round and round, as if bedevilled by the music. He looked again at the old men — there were three of them — and the young girl. One of their daughters maybe, or a grandaughter? He shaded his eyes again to look at her, but she was too far away to see in detail. He could smell the heady smell of mown grass, and the sweet fragrant smell of sunwarmed wood. Good smells, but he didn't feel good. Not bad either, but some peculiar feeling of longing he hadn't felt before.

He imagined walking over to the young girl, telling her that there were other things to do, taking her and leading her away, away from those old men. But then where would he take her? He watched as one of the old men threw the jack to start the next round. The girl stood behind the jack and began clapping her hands — why was she doing that? The next old man stooped and almost knelt down on one knee as he threw the first bowl. It curved in the wrong direction, then disappeared over the edge of the green. Archie laughed briefly, without humour, then turned and stepped into the shaded cool of the pavilion.

'Hi Starky.'

Starky's sandwich paused on the way to his mouth.

'Oho,' said Starky, 'so it's you, is it.' The hand with the

sandwich raised its index finger. 'Well if Ah've telt ye once Archie, Ah've telt ye a hundred —' Starky bit into the soft white bread, took a mouthful of tea, rolled all of it around in his mouth and swallowed with a muffled gulp. 'Ah've telt ye a *hunder* times: *mister* Stark's ma name, an that's what ye'll call me!' He stared at Archie from his watery eyes as he spoke. The mouth opened slowly and went for the sandwich.

'Been busy, mister Stark?'

'Mmmuh?'

Archie waited while the mouth filled up with tea, chewed loosely at solid and liquid alike, then swallowed all of it with a *glump*.

'Ho Ah've been busy aaright!' The thick finger prodded the air. 'It's aaright for some o us, eh? Yooz young yins on the dole! But some o us huff tae *work!*' Starky's eyes looked forgetfully at the sandwich. He hadn't said that very well. He took the last bite, drained his cup and smacked his lips. After a moment, he cleared his gullet softly and uttered: 'Ah've mowed that whole green, there's how busy Ah've been!'

'Any tea in the pot?' said Archie.

Starky ran a fat palm over his bald crown and declared: 'Oho, so now we know! Now we know what ye're efter!' Archie smiled and sat down on the edge of the table. From there he could look out of the little window and see the girl. She was flicking back her hair and clapping her hands again. 'An ye can take yer arse off o there,' said Starky, 'there's a seat, if ye want a chair.'

Archie pulled up a chair and sat down. Starky poured out two cups of thick dark tea, humming absently along with the accordian music. Suddenly the music stopped, and both looked at the radio. There was no sound apart from a faint crackle, then from outside the young girl's voice calling:

'Five feet . . . one o'clock.'

'What's she . . . ?' Archie began, but the radio announcer's voice interrupted him, apologising for the fault in transmission. The accordion music resumed, more demented than ever.

'Dead time,' said Archie.

'Ye what?'

'Dead time. It's what they call it, when there's nothing on the air.'

Starky raised his eyebrows and farted briefly.

'O I beg your —' He farted and chuckled simultaneously, then put a hand to his mouth to suppress an abrupt belch. 'Dead time is it now, well Ah've never in aa ma born days heard o that, it's a new yin oan me Archie.' He ran a palm over his baldness again and bit his lip. 'Ah've heard o *killing* time, mind you, but no this *deed* time ye're tellin me.'

'Killing time,' said Archie, sipping at the bitter, tepid brew, 'what does that mean Starky? Ah mean mister Stark.'

Archie knew what it meant, but asking him a question was a way of keeping the conversation from siezing up. Starky's face had gone blank with doleful consternation.

'Ye dinnae mean te tell me ye've never heard o *killing time*,' he said. He sucked up a mouthful of tea and grimaced as he swallowed it because it had gone cold.

'I've never heard of it,' said Archie. He tried to peer over the windowledge from where he sat, but it was too high.

'Well, it *means* —' Starky's eyelids fluttered slightly as he looked around the pavilion for a definition. This business of having to define the phrase seemed to make him lose all patience. 'Ach, it's an *expression* Archie, ye must ken it. It *means*. . . well *you* should ken what it means, ye *dae* it every bloody day: buggerin aboot oan that bike o yours, *that's* killin time! When ye could be *employin* yer time usefully lookin for *work*!'

As he spoke the accordion music became faster and faster, until Starky's patience ran out and he switched the radio off as he shouted the word *work*.

They heard the young girl's voice calling again: '*Two feet, at three o'clock.*'

'Which reminds me,' Starky resumed, 'ye can gie me a hand, if ye've nothing better tae dae bar killin time. Ye can gie me a hand wi they edges. They edges are still to be done.'

As Archie followed him out of the pavilion, Starky shook his head slowly from side to side and said, 'Aye, so ye never heard o killin time — Ah wonder what they've been teachin ye at school aa these years, eh?'

'Killing time,' said Archie, 'that's what they taught me.'

Starky chuckled laboriously and vented a series of high-pitched farts. 'O I beg your par. Ah dinnae ken. What's causin. Aa this flagellance. Ho Ah think ye're right there Archie, that's aa they dae teach yez nowadays.' Starky stopped outside the door. The thick finger prodded Archie's arm, then pointed towards the old men at the far side of the green. 'Did ye ever hear o anythin like that?'

Archie shrugged. 'Like what?'

Starky bent down slightly and brought his face so close to Archie's that Archie could smell the breath. There was amusement in his pale eyes as he spoke:

'Blind,' he said, 'every man jack o them, blind as bloody bats.' Archie turned his face away from the breath and looked over at the young girl. She was standing behind the jack and clapping her hands, waiting for the next old man to bowl.

'But she can't be —' Archie began, but Starky leaned closer and poked him softly on the shoulder and said:

'Partially sighted.' He went on, pleased that his revelation was having so much effect on Archie: 'They're frae the Blind Asylum. You watch.'

Archie watched one of the old men. He was saying something to his companions, and when he spoke he revealed a black gap between his eye-teeth, and when his face turned upwards Archie saw the shadowed, sunken eyelids. It looked as if his head were leaking darkness.

'You watch this,' said Starky, as the old man stooped and swung his arm back, throwing to the sound of the clapping. The bowl rolled slowly along the green, swung inwards and came to rest a long way in front of the jack. The girl stepped forward and bent down, seeming to gauge the distance between bowl and jack.

Starky nudged Archie gently in the ribs and said: 'Ye'd like tae get her in the bushes, eh? Whether she can see or no. That widnae make ony difference in the dark, hmmm?'

'*Seven feet, at six o'clock!*' cried the girl to the old men, then she took up her position behind the jack again and clapped her hands.

His dirty talk having failed, Starky chuckled and said: '*Dead* time, ye're tellin me aboot. Well . . .' he motioned loosely with a hand towards the girl, '. . . there's *blind* time for ye!' He ran his hand over his head and chuckled slowly. When he had finished and his humour had failed, he turned his watery gaze on Archie and said, 'Ye see, Archie, when she says *seven feet at six o'clock* like that, it's nothing tae dae wi *time*, really, it's aa tae dae wi the position o the *bowl*. A mean *six o'clock* means . . . well, if ye picture a clock, Archie, wi the jack in the middle —'

'Ah ken what it means,' said Archie. He was watching the next bowl travelling along the green. It swung inwards and slowed. It came closer than any of the others, close enough to enter her shadow. When it kissed against the jack, it made a small 'cloc'. The old men smiled and congratulated one another. Suddenly Starky began clapping his hands together loudly.

'Good bowl, marvellous!' he shouted.

At the sound of the loud clapping from another direction, all three of the men became confused and cocked their ears enquiringly. The girl peered over towards the pavilion.

Archie stepped down from the pavilion and climbed on his bike. Somehow the thought of the young girl, partially sighted herself, helping the blind old men to play bowls . . . it filled him with a strange disgust. He pushed down on the pedals and started cycling towards the gate.

'Hoi!' cried Starky, 'What aboot they edges?'

'Ah've got better things tae dae wi ma time!' Archie shouted without turning round.

'O ye have, have ye? Such as *what*?' cried Starky.

As he looked over his shoulder to glimpse the reddened, infuriated face of Starky, Archie stopped pedalling and felt the fixed wheel forcing his feet to go round and round.

'Nothing!' he shouted, then he picked up speed and swerved through the gate and rode away to do the Nothing.

The Shoes

ARCHIE NEWTON lifted out the inner bag, then undid the packet and flattened it out on the kitchen table. He laid one of his shoes on top, then drew a line around its sole with a biro. He did this twice on one side of the packet, then he turned it over and did the same with the other shoe. He sat down and started cutting out the foot-shaped pieces of cardboard.

'Ma, what time is it?' he shouted through to the living room. The television was on, and his mother did not hear him. He tried to fit the first piece of cornflake packet into his shoe, but it was too big. As he trimmed it with the scissors, he shouted again to his mother, but she didn't hear. He looked at the clock on the kitchen windowsill, but he wasn't sure if the time it told was the right time. It was the same little square blue clock his mother once tried to 'brain' him with. He'd been out with Jane, and hadn't come home till two in the morning.

He stopped what he was doing to laugh, remembering her with that clock in her hand, raising it high above her head and swearing she would *brain* him with it. She'd picked up the clock because it had been the nearest thing to hand, but now the picture in Archie's memory made him think she was blaming him for the passing of time itself. He shouted again, and when she didn't hear he felt annoyed and shouted louder:

'*Ma, what time is it?*'

His mother hurried into the kitchen and began to bang things around on the cooker.

'There's a clock there, isn't there,' said his mother.

'Is it slow or fast?'

'It's right as far as Ah know.'

'It's always wrong,' said Archie. He fitted the first foot-sized piece of cardboard into his shoe, then picked up the second piece and started trimming it with the scissors.

'Ah'm gonnae miss this bus,' said Archie.

'Ye will if ye dinnae hurry,' said his mother. 'Where is it ye're goin' anyway my lad?'

'Nowhere,' said Archie, 'just out.'

'Well mind and watch yersel,' said his mother, 'and don't be late.'

'Aye ma,' said Archie in a bored voice. He concentrated on fitting the second piece of cardboard into the shoe.

'What a mess in here,' said his mother, as she stepped between the foot-shaped pieces of cardboard on the floor. She poured hot water from the kettle over the dirty dishes in the sink and went on: 'Reminds me of the time we went ballroom dancing, me and yer faither.'

'Before ma time,' said Archie. He struggled to fit the third piece into his other shoe, then took it out and trimmed it with the scissors. 'Ma, Ah need a new pair of shoes!'

'There's a perfectly good pair in the hall,' said his mother. 'He'd only worn them twice before he died.'

'Ah cannae wear *them*,' said Archie, 'Ah need a *new* pair!'

'We'll just have tae see,' said his mother. She laid the cups to drain on the steel draining board.

Archie stood up and stamped his feet on the kitchen floor. He pulled on his jacket.

'Would ye look at this mess,' said his mother, picking up a few pieces of cardboard and the bag with the cornflakes in it.

'Ah'll have tae run for that bus,' said Archie. Out in the hall and with a hand on the front door, he heard her calling:

'You mind and watch yersel now, and don't be late!'

He shaded his eyes with a hand because of the sun coming through the window. He looked at the way her arm curved at the wrist when she poured the water. He'd never been alone with her in the house like this before. There had always been her mother, or her sister, or her big brother in another room. Usually she took him into the front room, the one the family never used. He wasn't used to being with her in the kitchen like this, and that was making it harder to tell her.

He sat and watched her face as she chattered and made tea and smiled at him, as if tonight was like any other night. Was she beautiful? He couldn't tell, her face kept moving. All he could tell was that her skin looked dark against the light from the window, dark but sort of glowing, and when she looked at him her eyes were very alive. The other thing he could tell was that he would never sit here and watch her like this again as she moved around the room talking and smiling, because even if he did it would be different. She was changing into a very beautiful person all the time, and if she was beautiful it was all to do with this changing thing. She was smiling at him a lot, and that was making it harder.

He looked out of the window and tried to concentrate on a little cloud above the rooftops. It didn't seem to be going anywhere or doing anything. It was that kind of evening, as if time wasn't passing.

'You take sugar?' she said, and she laughed because she'd never made tea for him in her house like this before and it was ridiculous.

'Two,' said Archie, then he laughed too because he had never had tea in her house like this before and it was ridiculous. It was all a bit like they were married, and that was making it harder.

'My mum used to make tea for my dad, before he died,' said Archie. He liked saying things to her which were dead obvious as if they were dead interesting.

'It would be strange if she did after,' she said, laughing loudly.

'She does sometimes,' said Archie, 'sometimes she pours out an extra cup.'

'Really?'

He liked making her laugh like that, then saying something that made the laugh change into really. And he wanted to kiss her because she was interested in the cup laid out for the dead, and because of the way her eyebrows went when she said really. But kissing her would only make things harder.

She came over to him and handed him a cup of tea. He put it on the floor beside his foot, then felt uncomfortable because of the shoes. It was a nice kitchen, nicer than in his house — it even had chairs a bit like armchairs, as well as the ones round the table —and every so often he remembered about the shoes. The big holes in the soles, the heels worn down almost to the uppers. The cardboard insoles he'd put in before leaving the house had worn through already, and now he could feel the new holes — holes in the holes. The last time he'd taken her out — to the pictures to see a D.H. Lawrence film — she'd noticed the shoes. He'd turned from the ticket-booth and seen her looking down at his worn heels, then she'd looked up at him and tried to hide it, but he'd seen the pity in her eyes. He'd felt angry about the pity, and hadn't started kissing her till half-way through the film. They'd gone on kissing for most of the second half, and he'd got his hand up inside her blouse, then down inside her jeans. She'd told him she loved him, but wanted to see how it ended.

Archie stared at his shoes: the heels were worn down even more now. He looked out of the window: the cloud had moved. He looked at her face: changing. Soon her mother would be back from work. He would have to tell her soon.

She curled up in a chair opposite him and eyed him and licked at her tea.

'You look like a cat when you do that,' said Archie.

'Do what?' she said. She licked at the tea again and grinned.

'That,' said Archie.

She yawned and stretched out an arm. 'Did you go to your nightclass last night?'

'Yeah.'

'What was it like?'

'Great. The teacher says I'll get an 'A'.'

'Then you'll go to Art College. D'you think you'll be a famous artist?'

Archie thought for a moment.

'Probably,' he said.

He was just about to cross his legs the way he had seen a famous artist doing it on t.v., with one ankle resting on the other knee, then he remembered about the shoes.

'I wouldn't talk to you if you were a famous artist,' she said. She came over to him and sat on the floor in front of him, leaning her elbows on his knees. He drew his feet as far under the chair as they would go. 'I wouldn't even come to the phone if it was you.' Her eyes had that look in them that said *so there*.

'How come?' said Archie, although he knew she wasn't really serious. They were never really serious when they talked about anything, they just talked and let the words take them somewhere.

'I'd chuck you,' she said.

'What for?' said Archie, playing along. But he knew that all this would only make it harder.

'I'd be too embarrassed. It would be like going out with *Eamonn Andrews*.' She laughed loudly about this, but stopped half-way when Archie didn't join in. And he knew that he would be laughing too if not for the shoes and the pity.

'But you'd say hello to me in the street!' said Archie, as if he was really serious.

'Well, I suppose I'd say hello in the *street!*' She laughed again, but stopped this time as soon as she'd started. 'What's wrong with you?' she said, frowning. She pulled away from him and frowned at him as if she were his mother. And he wanted to kiss her again because she was trying to frown and she didn't have the kind of face which could frown really. He said nothing, but leaned forward and stared at his cup of tea. She tugged at his sleeve. 'Hey, what's the matter with you tonight?'

'Nothing.'

'There is. What's wrong? You're not here.'

'How d'you mean?'

'You're not *here*,' she repeated, tugging at both his sleeves and trying to pull him into here. When that failed, she sat back and looked at him with narrowed eyes. She was good at narrowed eyes. It was one of those things Archie liked about her, all the crazy things she could do with her face. 'Look,' she said, in the tones of an offended auntie, 'ye havenae even *touched* yer tea!'

Archie looked at the undrunk cup of tea at his foot and suddenly felt like laughing out loud because it was ridiculous. Suddenly everything was ridiculous: this being in the kitchen together as if they were married; his mother telling him to 'mind and watch yersel' before he'd come out; the extra cup poured out for the dead; her saying it would be like going out with Eamonn Andrews. Everything made him want to laugh, everything was ridiculous. Everything except the shoes and the pity. He concentrated on the holes in his soles as a way of stifling the laughter. He waited for a minute, then he said it:

'I want to finish it.'

He'd wondered how it would sound when he said it. Now he'd said it, and he knew how it sounded. There was no beauty in it, and no pity. It sounded ordinary and ridiculous. He didn't look up, but heard her gasp.

'Why?'

When he did look up, he saw the first tear dripping from her eyelashes. She leaned forwards to put her arms round his neck, and the tear fell into his cup of tea. Then he could feel her mouth up against his ear and she was asking him why again. When she pulled away, her cheeks were wet with the tears.

'Are you fed up with me?'

'It's not that.'

'Why then?'

'It's just . . . time to finish it, that's all.'

'Time?'

She looked at the clock on the wall, as if the real explanation might be found there. Archie looked at it. It was the kind of clock his mother would have liked to possess.

'Who's that?' said Archie, as they heard the front door opening and someone come into the hall.

It was getting dark when Archie opened the door of the Boulevard Cafe in the High Street. He went in and saw Charlie there, sitting at the corner table they always sat at.

'Well,' said Charlie, 'how d'it go?'

Archie said nothing, but hung his head. He waited for the waitress to come, then ordered a tea.

'Did ye tell her?' said Charlie. Archie nodded and stared at the table. Charlie gave a long, low whistle. He was good at long, low whistles. 'Did ye pick the right time, the right moment?'

'There isn't a right time for it,' said Archie.

'Right enough,' said Charlie, 'But tell me what happened, eh? What did ye say? How did she take it?'

Archie shook his head and stared at the table.

'Okay,' said Charlie, 'tell me later.'

Both sat staring at the table until Charlie thought of something else to talk about.

'Hey,' he said, 'what d'ye think of these then?' He raised one leg above the level of the table, then pointed the toe of his shoe first one way, then another. He swung round in the seat and raised the other leg, so that both shoes were visible. 'Just got them the day. What d'ye thinka them? They're magic, eh?'

'Magic,' said Archie, without looking at the shoes. Then he did glance at them. They had cuban heels and chiselled toes and elasticated gussets down the insides, they were black and shiny and new, and he saw that they really were magic.

To Autumn

IT WAS AN ordinary October day in Edinburgh, the rain more or less incessant. Ernest Lovejoy — an unsmiling, unmarried and widely unpublished poet — was on his way home from his job in the public library when he realised that autumn had been underway for over a fortnight, and still no poem. His rain-stung fingers clenched around the polythene carrier-bag, which contained this week's ration of literature alongside the ingredients of a solitary bolognaise. Normally he'd have a sonnet on the go by now. Or, if he felt experimental, a *vers libre* 'Autumn', or even a sequence of haikus. At the very least, a prosepoem.

Last year — he gazed at the ground as he remembered it and saw, beneath his feet, all the motley leaves stuck to the wet stone like . . . *like* — he'd turned his hand to a very modern, almost concrete 'Autumn', in which a zigzagging arrangement of fragmented lines had been meant to suggest, mimetically, the leaves falling from the trees. No one could accuse him of being old-fashioned or unoriginal in *that* poem, though he would of course be willing to acknowledge the influences of Apollinaire, Dylan Thomas, e.e. cummings and possibly Lewis Carroll if the critics insisted. Those spiralling line-arrangements had been hell to type out — Lovejoy's typewriter was as old as Lovejoy, and just as temperamental — and then there had been all the problems involved in composing a suitably modern, up-to-date description of the season's change, taking great care of course to avoid all mention of trees. Each time he'd sent out that particular celebration of the earth's rhythm — four times, all told, then winter had set in — it had come back almost by return of post. A leaf determined to fall, with the editor's seasonal regrets.

Lovejoy grimaced at the ground — all those windblown, amber-bronze-golden leaves swirling round his feet like a . . . *like a* — as he recalled the remark one editor had thought him worthy of: *Promising. But too many similes, and too much alliteration.* Hadn't the man read Keats? And at Lovejoy's age — he was thirty-five, and keen on Conrad — that 'promising' had long since ceased to console. And now it was here again, season of mists and rejection-slips, just begging to be quatrained.

With his free hand he tugged the lapels of his jacket together, cursing the weather under his breath. With every step, the rain seeped up through his cracked soles, and every time he took a breath the icy wind did something onomatopoeic between his teeth. As he passed by a bookshop he slowed down and hesitated outside the door. The feeling of wanting to be inside, but at the same time reluctance to enter. Not that he didn't have the money to spare on a book — it was something worse than that. The pleasure Lovejoy took in browsing had palled, recently. Instead a strange sense of disgust, the word was not too strong, when confronted by all those regimented classics and those squadrons of paperback novels. Oddly enough this had not affected his work. The books in the library were, after all, only items to be numbered, catalogued and dusted. The ones on sale were somehow different, so much more challenging. Even the poetry section, with its slim and elegant editions of the living and its fat, complete works of the dead, no longer afforded Lovejoy consolation. At first he had told himself that he was appalled by the way literature had become so much a commodity — all those box-sets of Jane Austen and portable Hemingways for God's sake — but he knew that it was more than this. He knew that he was beginning to feel a keen despair with himself: with so much of the stuff already on the market, what could he, E. Lovejoy, hope to add?

A sequence of sonnets would be the thing. Establish himself with the traditional, the exciting new departures could come later.

Staring at the window display of best-sellers, Lovejoy caught sight of his reflection in the glass: too thin to be called slim, spineless in any case. The jacket plain, dogeared. The frontispiece of his face perhaps a reproduction of a print by Eduard Munch. Clearly destined to remain on the shelf, a book never to be reviewed. A limited edition of one.

He turned away from the bookshop — perhaps posterity would discover his manuscripts — and decided despite the weather and the hollow pain in his stomach to take the long way home through the park. Perhaps the small expanse of grass and sky, while barred clouds bloom the soft-dying etcetera, would spark off something. A couplet, maybe. Then he'd have something to work on after the spaghetti. This thought put a bounce into Lovejoy's step — his feet couldn't get much wetter — as he crossed the road and headed for the park. By the time its gates were in sight, he was already at work on it. Not the first draft perhaps, but very possibly the one *before* that, the one in the mind. His lips mimed the round-vowelled sounds which would soon become the syllables, then the words and the lines of the poem which, unless he was fooling himself, was very much imminent: 'To Autumn', by Ernest Lovejoy.

Maybe he was trying too hard.

More than half-an-hour had passed, slowly, with Lovejoy huddled in the shelter of the cricket pavilion, notebook in hand. Staring out at the rain there swaying in the wind, a thin veil over autumn's elusive face. Raindrops lining the roof's edge — the beads of her endless necklace. But nothing had come, not a word. The drab, dilapidated pavilion, daubed with gaudily painted gang-names, was beginning to depress him. Unfortunately it wasn't the right kind of depression, the kind which — he'd often heard it said — brought with it a muse. This was no such solemn, dignified emotion. This was an ordinary feeling of depression, a mere feeling of lack. What he needed was a good metaphor. He stared at a long line of cars passing along the road outside the park. How slowly, how monotonously those cars followed one another along, like the days of Lovejoy's life. He leaned back against the wall and closed his eyes and listened for the poem inside. The wind went on incanting her thin, meaningless vowel. The rain went on whispering her narrative on the roof.

No words came to Lovejoy.

Dropping the notebook and the pen, Lovejoy stood up and leaned against the wooden balustrade of the pavilion. He peered at a nearby tree. A tiny, bright red leaf came loose from a branch and was blown quickly towards him, landing a few inches from his foot. There was nothing very moving about the process as far as Lovejoy could see, if anything it looked slightly comical. If it made him feel anything at all, it wasn't the exquisite melancholy we associate with the perception of transience. He felt wet, and depressed, and ridiculous. As if through this so written-about phenomenon they called 'autumn', something or someone were poking fun at him. He had to concentrate, be serious.

What he needed was a personification.

Even the wind was distracting him from the task in hand. Running berserk among the shrubs like that. It wasn't exactly winnowing anyway. More like grabbing the trees by their throats and trying to throttle them. Picking up all the sodden leaves and throwing them around like that, like a lunatic. Suddenly Lovejoy sat down and picked up the notebook and the pen. He began to write furiously, words both momentous and illegible:

Wild wind, like a lunatic let loose —

For a moment he didn't quite know how to go on, but still. Quite a beginning. One more syllable and it might be the first line of a sonnet. He'd have to sort out the pentameters of course, get the thing to scan here and there. It was a fresh personification though, what with autumn as an escaped lunatic. All sorts of possibilities began to crowd into his mind. Winter as a group of male nurses, their icy eyes closing in on Autumn in the sestet somewhere. Lovejoy looked at the first line with dazed, admiring eyes. Then he heard, in the recesses of his consciousness, a small editorial voice: *Too many similes, and too much alliteration.*

'Hi there!'

Lovejoy closed the notebook with haste as he looked up. The girl — she looked like a student — swung her rucksack down beside him and began unbuckling the flap.

'Gee-zus, what rain! I'm *soaked*,' said the girl.

'It really is ah . . . raining, isn't it?' said Lovejoy, tucking the notebook into his jacket pocket.

'Raining! Man, it's *the Flood*.'

'Sometimes it's much worse than this here. During the winter it's —'

'If it gets any worse we'll need *snorkles*. Holy shit, it's like *Venice* without the *gondolas*. You waiting for the life-boat here, or what? Hey, you got a bottle?'

'Bottle? No, I —'

'Pity. I figured we could maybe send a message out, I mean like an SOS.'

Lovejoy watched in silence as she tugged a brown towel from her rucksack and began to dry her hair. She wore a maroon jerkin, a tight-fitting orange sweatshirt, brown corduroy jeans and a pair of beige leather boots. She was small, good-looking and there wasn't anything wrong with her. As his glances strayed from her face and hair to her shoulders and breasts, then down to her neat waist and hips, the word which came to Lovejoy's mind was *regular*. The only irregular thing about her seemed to be her eyes, which were green and very wide open, but which squinted a little. Perhaps it was the cat-like eyes which filled Lovejoy with hopeless longing. Or perhaps it was just that she was a regular American girl, come to him now in his hour of need, in the autumn of his youth, bearing the gift Lovejoy needed more than anything: words. He was aware that from time to time those green eyes were glancing at him between the dark hair and the towel. She expected him to say something more. Something interesting. They'd already covered the weather, and he sensed that to engage her for any length of time — a drink was already in his mind, then perhaps a candle-lit bolognaise for two — he'd have to impress her somehow.

The rain told its story on the roof, no words came to Lovejoy.

She threw the towel down on the top of her rucksack, sat down on the wooden floor, shuddered with the cold and pulled a packet of *Lucky Strike* from her jerkin pocket.

'You're ah . . . from America?' said Lovejoy. It wasn't much of a beginning, but perhaps the rest would follow from the first line. She nodded, lighting a cigarette, apparently waiting for him to continue. But in his mind Lovejoy was furiously scoring out that dull first line. That was the trouble with life, you couldn't revise it:

'Which part of the ah . . . States are you from?'

'I'm from Providence Rhode Island. My names Louise, what's yours?'

'Ernest,' said Lovejoy.

'As in Hemingway, huh?' said Louise, squinting mischievously. 'Well hi, Ernest, would you like a cigarette?'

'Please,' said Lovejoy, 'thanks.' As he took the cigarette, he glanced again at those eyes. It wasn't just the squint which made them unusual, but also the staring quality they had — wide open not with innocence or surprise but something much more permanent and durable. When she offered him a light, he wanted to steady her hand — not that it was unsteady, but it would be a touch, a trust — but his own hand somehow declined to make the contact. As always with Lovejoy, regrets were coming before the act. He thanked her again, inhaled deeply and gazed out over the park. He searched among the windblown leaves for his next line.

'Autumn,' he said, motioning loosely with a hand to the rain, the earth and the sky, 'always makes me fell a bit ah . . . melancholic.'

'Check,' said Louise, She blew a smoke-ring from her small mouth and added: 'I guess I interrupted you, huh?'

Lovejoy looked puzzled.

'Weren't you writing when I came along?'

'Oh, *that*,' said Lovejoy. He tried to smile nonchalantly. 'I was trying to.'

'You go right ahead and write,' said Louise, pointing with the lit tip of her cigarette to Lovejoy's jacket pocket. 'No shit, I won't disturb you.'

'It's all right, really, I don't want to.'

'You want me to go away?'

'O no! I mean acutally, well, as a matter of fact . . . I wasn't getting on too well with it.'

The green eyes stared at him squintly and with an intensity Lovejoy found unsettling.

'You a writer?'

This question had always brought a dilemma for Lovejoy. If he said yes, the next question would almost certainly concern his publisher. If no, he'd have to own up to his job in the library —hardly the sort of occupation to enthrall this girl from Providence Rhode Island, with her challenging green eyes, her *Lucky Strike*, her 'gee-zus' and 'holy shit'. Lovejoy therefore tried to sidestep the issue, nodding in a non-committal way, tilting his head a little to the side.

'You are?'

'Yes.'

'Who d'you write for?'

'Posterity.'

'I don't think I know it.'

Louise blowing smoke into the face of this late autumn afternoon, and the separate stares of her wide green eyes meeting on Lovejoy's mouth. Lovejoy still nervous about the question: to be a writer or not to be a writer? He had to change the subject fast:

'You're ah . . . on holiday here?'

Louise cleared her throat, flicked her ash and licked her neat red lips with the tip of her tongue. Lovejoy looked away, over the park to the queueing cars, unable to bear the desire that this peeping tongue aroused.

'Kinda,' said Louise. 'Kinda convalescing. See I was at Brown — that's the University in Providence. You heard of it? — and I was in my final semester, right? And wow, well it's a long story but I had this affair with my tutor. Okay okay, I know what you're thinking. You're thinking I'm stoopid, right? It was stoopid, the whole thing was all so *stoopid*. But when it happens it happens, right, so I fell in love with this creep. Boy, was he a creep. Turned out to be a mean little shit. O he was very *distinguished. Learned*, and all that crap. And very *respected* of course, by everyone including me till I realised what a *jerk* he was. He was a *writer* too, I even read all of his *books*! Anyway it didn't work out, of course — he was old enough to be my *father*, for Christ's sake — and so it fell apart. We didn't really have much in common I guess, except sex I guess. We *could* have, I really believe we coulda given each other a whole lot more, you know what I mean, but when it came down to it he didn't *wanna* have anything else in common. So all we did was fuck like snakes, till one day his *wife* found a tube of *ortho-cream* in the car. Don't get the wrong idea, we didn't actually *do* it in the *car* — it musta fallen outa my *bag* I guess. I wouldn't have minded so much if she'd found a *love letter* or something, but *ortho-cream* of all the shitty things. So she knew it wasn't *hers*, cause she'd been *sterilised* years ago. It made me feel kinda cheap. Just something to fuck if you know what I mean, something to *fuck* between his *seminars*, between chapter eight and chapter nine of his latest shitty *book*. That's what I was, I can see it now. Anyhow, in the end he went to his little wifeling with his little tail between his legs, promised *never* to be a *naughty* little professor *again*. And then they threw away that *nasty, horrible* tube of contraceptive jelly and lived happily ever after. The end. Meanwhile I went crazy. No kidding, the whole thing screwed me up so much I flunked my exams. Overdose, the whole scene. Made a shitty mess of *that* too. I took a year out and went to see an analyst, some Jungian nut with big hairy hands he kept *pawing* me with. Worked a coupla months in the library there in Providence, but shit was it boring, you know?'

'I know,' said Lovejoy.

'Heaving all those books around, boy that was *death*. Holy shit, you know what I used to do? I used to turn *his* books around, with the spines turned in so I couldn't even see the creep's *name*. That's how screwed up *I* was. So I quit, went to Italy and France. Then a coupla weeks in London. Caught a train up here. I'm going up north tomorrow. I guess I'll catch a train to Glasgow first, then head up there to the islands. Anyway here I am telling you my life story and drowning in this Scottish rain. So what d'you write anyway, Ernest? You a journalist?'

'O no,' said Lovejoy, still trying to assimilate the wealth of emotional data she had unpacked. 'No I write ah —' He had never been able to say it with complete nonchalance. Either it came out sounding pretentious, an extravagant lie, or as if it might refer to something unwholesome, something a grown man ought to keep under his hat. But there was no way round it: 'Poetry'.

In his mouth the word sounded more unfamiliar than ever, and faintly obscene.

'What kinda poetry?'

A difficult question for Lovejoy, he wrote so many kinds of the stuff. He leaned forward, elbows on knees, and stared at the ground. A mob of literary terms crowded into his mind, each shouting for his attention. He caught sight of the tiny red leaf the wind had blown to him earlier. He picked it up and held it between his fingers. What kind of poetry?

'Mostly the unpublished kind.'

To his immense relief, she laughed. What neat, regular little teeth. It wasn't much of a laugh, not quite a guffaw. But a little laugh was better than no laugh at all. Louise stubbed out her cigarette and laughed again.

'Hey, that's the *same kind* I write!'

Lovejoy managed a laugh too. Suddenly Ernest and Louise, the unpublished poets, had made contact through humour. as if to put this on record, they laughed again, this time in unison. When they had finished there was a new kind of silence between them. One they could share and relax with.

'Look at this,' said Lovejoy, holding out the scarlet, almost heart-shaped leaf in his palm. Louise leaned closer and picked the leaf out of his palm. Her green sphinxy eyes scrutinised it closely, then looked up.

'Mmm,' she said, 'it's neat.'

Things were looking neat for Lovejoy.

While he was in the bedroom, Lovejoy took the opportunity to make the bed. From time to time he stopped and stared for a moment at nothing, as if dazed. Was this really happening to *him*? Yes, it was. He was falling — not madly perhaps, and not without a sense of the folly of it, but falling all the same and grateful for it — in love with this green-eyed Louise. Finishing off the bed, he pulled his notebooks and folders from the drawer of his writing desk. He began to look through them. He wondered how he was doing — had she liked the meal? She had described it as sedating. Still, the conversation had gone quite well, and already in the living room the lights were low, the music soft. Lovejoy felt mellow, relaxed. The bottle of red wine Louise had bought on the way to the flat had certainly helped. After the meal, Louise had read some of her poems, all of which seemed to be addressed to the creep of a professor. She had asked him to read a few of his, and he had agreed. Leafing through the badly typed pages, he now wondered if this was such a good idea. Still, he'd come clean about his job and it hadn't made her jump up and call a taxi. If anything it had helped things along a little — it was, after all, something they had in common — but Lovejoy now wished he had steered the conversation from literature, especially his, and had kept it on the subject of sexual relationships, especially hers. What she had to say in that area intrigued him deeply, since his own experience of love-making had never involved a water-bed, a perineum —whatever *that* was — or the application of coconut oil.

He had never tried it the American way.

Collecting together the poems he'd picked out, Lovejoy consulted his image in the wardrobe mirror. Though his thinning hair had dried out, it still lay flat against his skull. His pink scalp shone through the gaps between the hair, which clung mainly to the sides of his head. He tousled it up, and returned to the living room. Louise had thoughtfully arranged a few cushions on the floor near the electric fire. Albinoni's violins wept from the stereo, and generally the room had an atmosphere Lovejoy had never been able to create on his own.

'Mind if I roll one?' said Louise. He noticed that she had in her hand a polythene bag filled with dried leaves.

'What is it?' said Lovejoy. He sat down awkwardly on the cushions and peered at the bag of leaves.

'Columbian,' said Louise. 'It's good.'

Lovejoy shrugged, smiled and nodded all at once. Though he'd heard of it of course, and had sometimes caught its aroma at parties, he'd never actually tried it. Still, he didn't wish to appear old-fashioned or stuffy. Anyway, what the hell, he was in the mood for a new experience.

'Are you sure you ah . . . want me to *read* them?' he said. 'You wouldn't rather look at one or two yourself?'

I'd like it oral,' said Louise, rolling the dark grass into a long paper printed with a tiny version of the stars and stripes. Lovejoy watched, enchanted by the inch of tongue with which she licked its gummed edge.

'Aren't you going to ah . . . put some tobacco in too?'

'You read the poems, I'll roll the sticks. Okay?'

Lovejoy nodded and shuffled through his pages. He pulled out one and looked it over, biting his lip.

'I suppose I could read this one, if you like.'

'What's it's name?' Louise lit the American flag fat with leaves and passed it to Lovejoy.

'Autumn in the city,' said Loveyjoy.

'Shoot.'

He cleared his throat, reannounced the title, then took a few deep inhalations of the sweetly smelling smoke. To begin with he read the lines nervously and too quickly. He had never read anything aloud like this before. Soon, however, his own voice seemed to swell and resonate around the words. The words themselves seemed to be charged with a power he had not suspected of them, and there was nothing for it but to let the words take over. Between poems Louise said nothing, but passed him the long smoking thing and urged him to read the next. After a time, she lay back on the cushions, closed her eyes and apparently let the words take over too. Lovejoy went on reciting, his voice rich with implication. Suddenly, half way through a quatrain, something strange began to happen. He no longer understood the words. Their sounds became ominous, and ridiculous, and all sorts of other things. It was as if their history, the sum total of their usages and associations, had become somehow actual and present as he uttered them. They danced along the page before his eyes, a cryptic script he could no longer decipher, an algebra of lyricism he could barely remember how to pronounce. He did not understand, either, why he had written all this down in the first place, nor why he was now reading it aloud to a stranger who appeared to be falling asleep on the living room floor. He stumbled, and stopped on the word 'now'.

After a moment Louise stirred, opened her eyes and yawned.

'Mmm,' she said, 'you wanna know what I think? I think it's got a lotta potential, but . . . You wanna know what it reminds me of?'

'Keats,' said Lovejoy abstractedly.

'Well, yeah. A lotta stuff about the fall. And that one about the nymph, that nymph in the garden, you know. I guess that was kinda Keatsian.'

'Did you think there was too much ah . . . simile? Alliteration?' said Lovejoy, still intrigued and slightly alarmed by the sound and the power of each word as he uttered it.

'Maybe there was, yeah. But you wanna know what it reminded me of? My father. See I was never too close to my father, I guess. It's a long story but anyway, he was an alcoholic. Boy, was he an alcoholic. Anyhow, I never really felt I had a father. He was always leaving or going in somewhere to dry out, you know? So I guess I didn't see much of him. Even when I did see him, he wasn't *there*, if you see what I mean. He was somewhere else. Which is why I probably got stuck on that *jerk* of a professor. I guess I kinda needed a surrogate. Anyhow, my father painted pictures, right, he was an artist or so he thought. A few other people thought he was too, so they bought his pictures. Which was the worst thing they coulda done, if you ask me. Anyway, your poems kinda reminded me of my father's pictures, you know? 'Cause every one is like it's been written by a different person, sort of. I mean, you walk into my mother's apartment and it's like the History of Art, volumes one to twenty. Giotto to Jackson Pollock, the whole caboodle. Cubism, fauvism, expressionism, every stoopid old ism you can think of. It's all there on the walls, every style and technique there is. Everything except him, you know?'

'I know,' said Lovejoy sadly.

'You do?'

'Sure,' said Lovejoy, surprised a little by his use of the word, 'you mean none are genuine. None of your father's paintings, and none of my ah . . . poems.'

'Well, I wouldn't say *that*,' said Louise, propping herself up on one elbow and opening her eyes full. 'Don't get me wrong, I'm not trying to be critical or anything. I liked some and I wasn't so keen on some others, but mostly they just kinda reminded me of a whole lotta other poems. I mean there's nothing *wrong* with that. You gotta have some influences, but you've gotta find your own kinda . . .'

'I never have,' said Lovejoy, and the words seemed to well from a deeper source than the one which had given rise to his poetry.

'You *will*,' said Louise, 'if you really want to.'

He knew that normally he would finish such an appraisal wounding. Tonight he wanted to hear it, the truth. He smiled, then giggled a little. Louise responded by smiling back at him. Lovejoy laughed out loud. Inside, he felt a peculiar radiance spreading through his limbs, as if his cells were alight, as if somewhere inside him a younger, more agile, and much stronger man were stretching, rippling and getting ready to come out. Perhaps it was this inner man who stretched out a hand and ran a finger down the side of Louise's face, lightly stroked her neck, her shoulder, her breast.

Louise whispered something in his ear about a cap, her mouth so close to his ear that the words became a caress.

Lovejoy awoke to the abrupt noise of the front door closing. He felt groggy, and as if he had aged considerably during the night. He coughed harshly, then gulped down the bitter phlegm. What variety of passions he had partaken of, what inventive intimacies, what prolonged pleasures with Louise! But where was Louise? Had she gone without a goodbye?

He stumbled out of bed and, noticing the clock, realised that he was hopelessly late for work. But this was not the point, the point was Louise. He staggered to the window and caught sight of her, pack on her back, dark hair blown back by the wind, turning the corner out of the street. Perhaps he could catch her, if he hurried? But then, what would be the point? She had decided to go. He stood by the window for a few moments, staring absently at the sunlight flashing from a puddle of dirty water. Was this what a poet would call sweet sorrow? In any case he felt it keenly, but also felt a pressing need to piss. Naked, Lovejoy walked to the toilet and listened with closed eyes to the rattle of his water in the bowl.

In the living room he found her note, propped up against the empty wine bottle:

Dear Ernest,

Tried to wake you up, but I guess you'd gone into hibernation for the winter. Hope you don't hate me for running off like this, I decided to go book a flight. I figure I'll do my final year again when I get back, get myself straightened out. Maybe see you again sometime — who knows, maybe I'll visit Scotland again next fall. Everything changes, I guess.

See ya,
crazy Louise.
X X X

P.S. You gotta keep on writing, Ernest. Start with this.

A long arrow trailing down to the bottom of the note. On the table lay the tiny, scarlet leaf. Lovejoy picked it up and stared at it in wonder, confounded by its tiny shape, its tiny colour, and by the feel of its tiny flesh between his fingers, unlike anything else in the world.

A Little Bit of Repartee

THERE WERE eighty-eight of them. Larry had polished eighty-seven — his moment of satisfaction had come. He picked up the last one and looked at the swollen little image of himself in its surface. 'Piglet,' said Larry. He raised it to his nose, sniffed and said: 'The bouquet is rather pretentious, but . . .' He steamed it with his breath, polished it deftly with the soft cloth, then looked again at the bloated little replica of himself and smiled. '. . . but on the whole a full-bodied little fag.' He placed it with the others, on the bar beside the flowers, then looked at all eighty-eight of them. 'There,' said Larry.

He gathered eight up by their stems and took them to a table. Between his fingers they looked like bubbles. He put them in their places carefully, as if they might burst. When he'd placed all eighty-eight glasses on the tables, he stood in the centre of the restaurant and looked around. He caught sight of himself in the alcove mirror. He turned this way and that, tugging the points of his waistcoat down and inhaling deeply. Without breathing out, he sucked in his cheeks.

'Not fat,' he said, letting out a little of his breath. 'Rather say plump. Not corpulent,' he said. A little more of his breath escaped. 'Hardly obese.' He exhaled completely and saw the figure in the mirror sag. 'You fat little fag you,' he said.

He looked at his watch and rolled his eyes. 'Time for the *candles*,' he said.

From his waistcoat pocket he tugged a squashed box of matches, struck one and cupped his hands around it. He lit three candles with the first match, shuffling hurriedly from one table to another. He lit four with the second match, one with the third match and the last three candles with the fourth match. He pulled the order pad from his hip pocket and turned it over, then wrote the number four on the back of the pad. He added up the little column of numbers and wrote down the total.

'Not bad, he said. 'An improvement on last week at least.'

He walked to the window, leaned on the coffee machine and gazed through the tinted glass. At the place over the street, the little Indian waiter was standing at the window, looking out. Larry put his hand to his mouth to cover a falsetto giggle. It sounded like a little boy being tickled. Larry then waved to the Indian waiter just as the door opened and Eddie walked in.

'I've told you about that before,' said Eddie. 'You promiscuous little bitch, d'you think he can see you through that sunglass?'

'It makes me look darker, that's all,' said Larry. He stuck out his tongue at Eddie and waved again, even though the little Indian waiter had turned away.

Eddie hung up his Maigret raincoat and sat at the alcove table. He slipped off his shoes, which were duck-egg blue, then took a black leather pair from a carrier-bag.

'Are they ready in there?' said Eddie, nodding to the kitchen at the rear of the restaurant.

'Chicken isn't quite defrosted yet,' said Larry, 'but when is it ever? We should really put it on the menu you know, Salmonella a la King.' He looked at Eddie for the smile, but Eddie didn't give him one.

'Are they all here?' said Eddie.

'Of course they're all here,' said Larry, 'it's ten-past eight for heaven's sake!'

Larry stood with his feet apart and his hands on his hips — a cartoon of the wife scolding her husband for his lateness.

Eddie took a shoe-horn from his bag as he looked up.

'D'you do alarm calls too?' he said.

'Ho ho ho,' said Larry. He drummed his fingers on his hips and tried to raise an eyebrow.

Eddie looked up again, the shoe-horn in beside his heel. In the candle-light his complexion looked smooth and unreal, like the glow of wax fruit.

'Tell me something, Larry,' he said, 'are you fond of children?'

Larry closed his eyes and sighed emphatically. 'Yes,' he said, 'but I've learnt to cultivate geraniums instead.'

'I was just thinking Christmas is coming,' said Eddie. 'You could always get a job as a santa.'

Larry sat down at the table, the better to ignore Eddie at close quarters. He did so now as pointedly as he could, folding his arms huffily and averting his eyes. When he sensed that he'd got

Eddie's attention, he did an Over-The-Shoulder-Withering and said: 'Ho, ho, ho.'

Eddie prodded him in the midriff with the shoe-horn and said: 'There you are, you see? You're doing it again, that ho ho ho. You'd be very good as santa!'

He prodded Larry's bulge with the shoe-horn again and added: You've got the belly for it all right.'

'This is mental cruelty, you know,' said Larry. He averted his weight, crossing his legs the way a thin person might. The chair whined a little. 'Just because I'm a little overweight, there's no need to treat me like the The Elephant Man. Actually, I've come to terms with it — I've come to the conclusion that my weight problem, as you insist on calling it, is purely and simply a matter of . . . eating far too much of the wrong things.' He nodded at Eddie with finality, as if to say *so there*. After a moment, he added: 'See? I've virtually got it under control.'

Eddie looked at himself in the alcove mirror, smoothed an eyebrow with a licked fingertip and pursed his lips. He lit a cigarette and placed it between his lips, all the time eyeing his own image in the mirror, turning his face this way and that.

'It wouldn't be so much of a problem if you cashed in on it,' he said.

'Oh, leave me and my weight problem alone!' said Larry, crossing and uncrossing his legs, making the chair whine and whine. He looked at Eddie then copied what he was doing — lit a cigarette, looked at the mirror, sucked in his cheeks. 'We can't all be thin, handsome, and *conceited*. Some of us have to be fat and funny and *nice*. We all have our different roles in life, Eddie dear, you should know that by now.' He nodded a *so there* at Eddie and smiled at himself in the mirror.

'That's what I'm saying,' said Eddie. 'It's your role in life I'm concerned about.' Eddie let the smoke unravel itself from his lips, all the time consulting his own eyes in the mirror. He smoothed his hair with the palm of his hand, glanced at Larry's reflection and added: 'A santa.'

Larry stood up abruptly, then bent down to pick up Eddie's blue shoes. He put them in the carrier-bag and shuffled hurriedly over to the coat-hooks. He hung up the bag under the Maigret raincoat and said:

'Santa my arse.'

Eddie took the nail-file from his waistcoat pocket and began to file the nail of his pinkie, humming to himself and looking aloof. Larry shuffled back to the table and sat down. He looked at what Eddie was doing, then made the most of rolling his eyes.

'All I'm saying,' said Eddie, moving on to the next finger, 'is that people like us have to make the most of it. Our weakness. Our little weakness.' He tapped Larry's creased and bulging waistcoat with the nail-file, then went on presenting the mirror with his profile, watching himself draw deeply on the cigarette.

The words hurried out of Larry's mouth: 'Oh it's weakness, is it? Listen to Narcissus! Well what about *your* little weakness —and I don't mean *that* . . .' He glanced quickly at Eddie's lap. '. . . I mean did you call in anywhere tonight, on the way to work? I mean did you stop off at a *bar*, by any chance?'

Eddie spread out the fingers of the hand he'd been doing and pursed his lips judiciously.

'I called in somewhere,' he said, lightly, 'for a little one.'

Larry slumped in his chair, closed his eyes and tried to look sincerely disgusted. He began singing in a small voice:

'One man went to mow, went to mow a meadow . . .'

'Oh, don't start that!' said Eddie, 'I admit I had a couple.'

Larry paused to clear his throat sarcastically before continuing: 'Two men went to mow, went to mow a meadow . . .'

'Three!' said Eddie, between his teeth, 'Now be a good girl and stop it!' He began filing the nail of his other pinkie.

Larry kept his eyes closed, tapped out the rhythm with a finger and went on singing in the small voice: 'Three men went to mow, went to mow a meadow. Three men, two men, one man . . .'

Eddie threw the nail-file on the table, stubbed out his cigarette and clapped his hand over Larry's mouth, but the little voice went on singing.

'Three men, two men, one man and his dog, went to mow a meadow . . .'

'I had four drinks!' said Larry, 'now stop it, will you?'

When the little voice had stopped singing, Eddie took his hand away from Larry's mouth, grimaced at the wet on his palm and wiped it on a serviette.

'You know I can't stand you and your men going to mow,' said Eddie. 'It's as bad as that game you play with the matches and the candles — you're a bag of phobias, you are! You're a nervous wreck, a catastrophe!'

'It's important to keep track of things!' said Larry.

'Keep track of things!' said Eddie. 'Keep track of things! Why on earth is it important to keep track of how many matches you use to light the candles, for God's sake?'

Larry, unable to answer, endeavoured to raise an eyebrow in disdain. The other eyebrow moved too and his balding scalp edged forward a little — his whole face, and even the lobes of his ears, seemed to be set in motion by the effort to raise an eyebrow.

'What on earth are you trying to do now?' said Eddie, smoothing his hair with his palm and raising an eyebrow easily.

Larry forgot his own reflection and turned to Eddie. He gave him the let's-be-honest-with-each-other stare. For a moment they looked into one another's eyes.

'Five?' said Larry.

'Four,' said Eddie.

'Truth?' said Larry.

'Absolutely,' said Eddie.

'So,' said Larry, '*four* little drinks on the way to work. Eddie, my dear, you are an al-co-hol-ic. I am living — and working —with an al-co-hol-ic. I wouldn't be surprised if I'm asked to take part in a documentary on the subject. The plight of the wives. I'll be interviewed in silhouette, I can see it now. D'you think I've got the profile for it?'

'Your profile would fill the screen,' said Eddie, giving Larry's belly a dirty look, 'and it would be a different documentary: Obesity, the facts and the fantasy!'

Larry made a hurt face: 'Be *nice* to me!'

Eddie curled his lip and looked Larry up and down. 'Nice!' he sneered. 'I'm sick to the back teeth of you and your "*nice*".'

Larry slouched and pouted at himself in the mirror. He looked up at Eddie with big eyes, as a dog would its owner.

'It's only oral gratification,' he said.

'It's unadulterated gluttony,' said Eddie, 'and talking about gratification, while you were out to lunch with that little Indian tart, I was at home feeling very frustrated, lonely and depressed. I had a bath, went to bed and resorted to something I haven't done for a long time!'

'Oh don't say that word, Eddie, please!' said Larry, screwing up his eyes and putting his hands over his ears, 'It always makes me think of muzzled dogs!'

'What on earth d'you mean,' said Eddie, 'what word?'

Larry mouthed the word silently and shuddered.

'Oh, I didn't resort to that!' said Eddie. 'No, I resorted to watching Crossroads. I took the TV into the bedroom.'

'Crossroads?' said Larry, rounding his eyes in horror, 'that's even worse! Why on earth did you do that?'

'Call it a wild impulse,' said Eddie. He lit another cigarette and placed it on the rim of the ashtray, then loosened his collar and began massaging his own neck with both hands. 'It was either that or . . . muzzled dogs.'

'A wild impulse,' scoffed Larry, 'watching Crossroads!'

'Oh, all right,' said Eddie, 'it was a premeditated act of self-abasement.' He picked up a cigarette and took it between his lips, then he tightened his collar and rearranged the tie.

Larry went into an elaborate fit of the giggles. He doubled up and moved around on the chair laboriously, making it whine repeatedly. He put his hand over his mouth, but the giggles hurried out between his fingers. His face reddened, and beads of sweat began to stand out on his forehead. When he had finished, he dabbed his eyes with a serviette, then blew his nose into it.

'Oh, I like a good giggle,' he said, 'a little bit of repartee before the hell begins.'

Eddie dropped his cigarette into the ashtray without bothering to stub it out. He stared at Larry, apparently appalled. He let his head droop until it rested on his arm, then made a noise in his throat which sounded like a stifled sob.

'What's the matter with you?' said Larry. 'I mean apart from you vanity, your alcoholism and your traumatic adolescence?'

Eddie banged the table with the flat of his hand, making the cutlery jump a little. Larry let out a small squeal of fright.

'Hell! Hell!' said Eddie, staring at himself ominously in the mirror.

'Have I said something, by any chance?' said Larry. Eddie didn't reply, but went on staring at his reflection.

Larry improvised a series of artificial coughs while he waited, then sighed emphatically and stubbed out Eddie's cigarette.

'Sorry I spoke, I'm sure!' he said, turning away from Eddie and emitting a small, whimpering noise.

'Oh, for Christ's sake shut up!' shouted Eddie. 'You're not my pet poodle, you know! You're a human being! A grown-up human being!'

Larry cut the whimpering and looked at Eddie, surprised and doubtful. He opened his mouth to speak but said nothing.

Eddie went on staring. 'I'm depressed as hell,' he said. 'No, no, that's not it, it's worse than depressed. It's that nothing feeling. The feeling that nothing's happening, nothing's ever going to happen. Even if it did, it wouldn't be *real*. We're actors, that's all, except that we don't have a play, a stage . . . we've got the walk-on parts every night, the waiters, we're not expected to be people. The more like machines we are, the better we are at our part. Yes sir, certainly sir, allow me to adjust you bib. Would you care for dessert, perhaps the cheeseboard? What would I recommend, sir? Why, for those who can't make up their own minds I recommend breast-feeding, sir, but even then there's a choice involved! It makes me sick!'

Hesitantly Larry laid his hand on Eddie's arm, took a quick breath as if about to speak but again said nothing.

Eddie ignored the hand. He went on staring at himself murderously and talking:

'No wonder I drink too much! It's the same, night after night, the same actions. It goes on and on, but none of it means anything. Even when we talk, we don't *say* anything! You said it yourself —it's just a little bit of *repartee*!'

Larry the concerned parent, raised his hand to Eddie's shoulder and patted. In a soft voice, he said: 'Well? What's wrong with that?'

Eddie shrugged the hand away and spread out both his own hands, the nail of each elegant finger glinting in the candle-light. 'Doesn't it bother you that we don't actually . . . *talk*? Get *through* to each other?'

'We hurt each other's feelings, sometimes,' said Larry, brightly.

'Ach, you don't know what I mean,' said Eddie, lighting another cigarette with exaggerated nervousness.

Larry did a long-suffering sigh and rolled his eyes.

'I do know what you mean,' he said. 'You mean our conversation follows a predictable pattern, meaningless in itself, or jest and rejoinder.'

'Oh for crying out loud!' He flicked his ash repeatedly, though there was none to flick. He flapped a hand at the mirror and added: 'Look at us! We're caricatures!'

Larry patted his bulging waistcoat with both hands and said: 'Let's just say we're larger than life.'

'Some a whole lot larger than others,' said Eddie, as pointedly

as he could. After a moment he added: 'You see? Here we go again
— the double-act! It's as if we've learnt our lines!'

'But I love you!' whined Larry. 'And that isn't in the script!'

Eddie smiled slightly, consulting his image in the mirror, then
turned to Larry and said: 'I lie to you too sometimes.'

'That's the idea, a rejoinder,' said Larry. After a few moments
of silence, he stood up and said, 'I suppose it's time we were open.'

Eddie stood up, collected the ashtray he'd been using and the
soiled serviettes. 'With each other, you mean?' he said, walking
towards the door into the kitchen.

Larry groaned, on cue. He looked at himself in the alcove
mirror. 'Oh Eddie my dear,' he said, 'd'you really think I'd make a
good santa?' As Eddie opened the kitchen door he called over his
shoulder: 'Devastating.'

Larry pushed out his belly.

'Ho, ho, ho,' he said. He shuffled hurriedly to the door and
turned the sign around so that it said 'closed' on the inside.
'Open', said Larry. He stood at the window and looked out
through the tinted glass to the window across the street. The
little Indian waiter wasn't there. Outside, a young couple stopped
to read the menu. Larry turned to survey the tables, then put a
hand to his mouth.

'You forgot the *flowers*!' he said in a scolding tone.

He hurried behind the bar and found the flowers where he had
left them. He unwrapped them, then clipped their stems with a
small pair of nail-scissors. He placed each one in its slender glass
vase, then carried them to the tables. When he'd placed one in the
centre of each table, he stood in the middle of the restaurant and
looked around.

'There,' he said.

Table D'hote

MARIA SITS opposite Eric, not drinking her wine.

She has raised her glass and now she holds it there, just a little below her chin. Soon she'll drink, or put the glass back down on the table, but not yet. For the moment she'll go on looking across the table at Eric, watch him as he fidgets with his glass, his knife, his serviette.

How did it happen? Be honest, Eric.

Now the hand can resume its mission, tilting the glass as it carries it to the mouth. Maria's lips take the rim of the glass at last, the more eagerly for having been made to wait. She drinks.

Eric sits opposite Maria, not drinking his wine.

He is looking down into his glass. He tilts the glass from side to side, making his reflected face change shape. In the red wine his features distort. Drunk again — was that how it happened? He looks up at Maria, for a moment confronts that trusting, candid stare. Be honest.

I met her. I kept meeting her, bumping into her.

Eric's hands begin a restless, evasive gesture above the flowers, the little vase of flowers on the restaurant table. When Maria looks at the hands, the hands begin to feel foolish. They catch hold of one another, retreat behind the flowers, but no —they can't hide there. At length Eric knits his two hands together and places them on his place-mat, where he'll endeavour to make them stay. His head is bowed, and all in all it looks very much as if Eric might be about to say grace. *For what we are about to receive* . . . that's how it happened, those restless hands.

One night I met her at a party, a party at Frank's.

Cleverly Eric pauses to let the name resonate. If he were to think aloud now he would say: *Frank — remember him, Maria? The one you said had hairy shoulders.* Instead he pauses, sniffs at the bouquet of the wine despite the fact that it has none, takes a civilised sip, winces, then throws his head back and drains the upturned glass.

Maria, meanwhile, watches his Adam's apple pulsate. It reminds her oddly, of a fish — the opening and closing of gills. When Eric puts down the glass she sees the mouth: it pouts, smacks its lips, smiles. She finds herself addressing his teeth:

How long ago was this?

Eric's smile becomes less than a smile, then vanishes. The lips form an O-shape, and the initial vowel disintegrates into words:

Only a few weeks ago. When you were in London, and.

And so Eric, wearily, recounts the events by which he and Lillian became lovers. How they met that night at Frank's party, danced for a time together, drank far too much wine, retired to the room being used for coats in order to smoke a little joint and talk about . . . but what had they talked about — *relationships?* Occasionally he glances at Maria, and from the sceptical look in her eyes it is clear that none of this explains how anything happened. But how is Eric to convey it? The atmosphere of lust and romance, the excitement of the banal music, the drunkenness and the drugs, the tacit intimacy behind the sordid procedure? Especially in a restuarant and besides . . . how the memory dissembles! Because that night wasn't the night, not the night that he and Lillian.

Eric interrupts his narrative to pick at his teeth with a toothpick, though the starters haven't come yet. He extricates a morsel of breakfast, examines it closely then discards it. To avoid Maria's eyes (be honest, Eric) he stares into the alcove beyond her shoulder, where the ornamental mirrors on the wall slice his image into two. By moving his head a little this way and that, he plays at making his face fragment and then reform. Best keep it simple.

Then I went back to her place for coffee, and.

And Eric's hands come to life again: one tugs a cigarette from the packet, while the other swoops for the bottle and, catching it, offers it to Maria. Maria's hand holds out her glass, while Eric's hand tilts the bottle and pours. Maria's other hand lights the lighter and offers the flame to Eric's other hand, the hand with the cigarette. His hand steadies hers as he takes the light. Both watch with distrust the hands which go on serving one another regardless, parting and coming together, regardless of how it happened.

Maria, exhaling two jets of blue smoke from her nostrils, begins to examine her fingernails impatiently. Realising that the story — this tale of the unexpected: How Eric And Lillian

Happened — is lacking still its denouement, she decides to prompt the teller:

Is she good in bed?

Eric spills a little wine as he puts down his glass. He studies his hands, the cigarette, the red stain growing on the white tablecloth. He smiles sorrowfully at his drink, unwilling to lie to Maria. Reluctant, also, to be honest. His one-eyed reflection stares up at him from the wine, a gloomy fish. Eric shrugs his shoulders.

Yes.

Maria begins to suffer.

Sooner or later someone will have to say something. The starters, inedible as they were, have been eagerly consumed. The wine too has come in useful and Eric has already ordered a second bottle of the same. And everything is going smoothly but for the fact that silence has joined the two at the table. On the one hand Maria ought to say something since it is, strictly speaking, her turn. On the other hand Eric ought to qualify that fateful *yes* of his. A little smalltalk is all that is required, but neither is able to provide it.

At the next table, quite the contrary situation has come about: a young, well-dressed couple, having opted immediately for the *a la carte* menu, now discuss animatedly which dishes to select. But then there are so many to choose from, and clearly they have so many other things to talk about, that the young man calls to the waiter and orders a bottle of champagne to be going on with. The young lady expresses her delight by blowing the young man a little kiss over the table. The young man responds by taking her hand and squeezing it gently.

Maria, turning her eyes from the kiss-blowing and hand-squeezing, begins to brood on the fact that she and Frank, during their brief but exhilarating affair, dined out only once, decides to ask Eric how often he and Lillian have eaten out. It is a way of estimating how far things have gone.

Eric, how often have you and Lillian . . ?

But Eric averts his eyes to see the waiter at his side, presenting the second bottle of the same bad wine for inspection. Eric nods, smiles. Carefully then the waiter unpeels the seal, places the bottle on the table, begins the slow ritual of uncorking the wine.

Everything all right, sir?

Eric affects nonchalance as he utters his *uh huh*.

Easing the cork soundlessly from the bottle, with neither Eric nor Maria caring to disturb the silence, the waiter proceeds to refill each of the glasses. At length he lays the bottle down between them and, before he departs, makes a few small alterations to the arrangement of the objects on the table — the little vase of flowers a little more to the side, the pepper and the salt a little closer together, the ashtray out of sight behind the flowers. He makes a slight bow before he turns to depart. Eric nods, smiles.

Alone together again, Eric and Maria pick up their glasses and drink in unison. It tastes better than the first, and Eric looks at his glass appreciatively as he resumes the conversation:

Slept together? A few times, quite a few.

He picks up his knife and tries to balance it on his finger, but it tilts this way and that precariously. He looks forgetfully at Maria, pities her: sipping her wine, frowning slightly, twisting and untwisting a lock of her hair between her fingers. She appears so forlorn, suddenly, that Eric feels within himself an irresistible rush of affectionate regret. Regrettably, his knife rebounds off the side-plate and falls to the floor. The couple at the next table look over briefly, then away. Eric dives, begins to grope around Maria's shoes. Retrieving the knife and on the way back up, he is stunned momentarily by the apparition, between skirt and stockingtop, of her soft, corallaceous thigh.

Maria looks with pity at the bald spot on the crown of Eric's head as he climbs back on board the table. His face is flushed, his breathing harsh, and for a moment he looks simply old and exhausted. Maria finds herself offering him a cigarette, and though the question she asks is a difficult one, the tone of her voice is warm and consolatory:

Are you in love with her, Eric?

Eric does not know, or is unwilling to state the answer. He looks over his shoulder to the kitchen — surely the main course must be on its way by now. He scratches his chin impatiently, rubs one of his eyes, makes the most of blowing his nose, but no —it still hasn't come. He picks up his knife, puts it down again, then hazards a kind of guess:

I'm fond of her. I don't know . . .

His hand goes for the bottle, picks it up and waves it around a little — a gay gesture, but done with sorrow. Maria offers her empty glass, and as Eric refills it her wrist begins to sag with the weight of the wine.

You make it sound like a misfortune.

Eric manages to smile and frown simultaneously at this acute observation, but when the smile goes the frown remains, and it is with a bitter curl of the lips that he replies:

Isn't it?

As if to reassure herself that love need not be a misfortune, Maria glances at the couple at the next table. Their conversation has paused, but somehow they give the impression that even silence is a kind of sharing. She turns to Eric, watches him smoke his cigarette. How he prevaricates even with that: worrying at the ashtray with it, rolling it around in his fingers, tapping his lips with the tip . . .

So what are you going to do, Eric?

Eric's lips droop to the rim of the glass. As he gulps the wine a thin trickle escapes from the corner of his mouth and meanders down his chin. He dabs his face with the paper serviette, shrugs.

I'm not sure . . . what to do.

Eric takes the paper serviette and begins to do some origami. He makes a triangular fold. Perhaps a little boat? His fingers fidget with the sail, tugging and pressing. When it is finished, he places it in the little harbour between his knife and his fork. Maria watches Eric's thoughtless finger push the little boat out of the harbour, around the salt-cellar light-house, out into the open table. Looking away, she sees that the waiter is approaching and yes, the main course has arrived at last.

Sooner or later, Eric, you'll have to decide.

And as the waiter lays out the clean plates he suppresses a yawn and once again enquires:

Everything all right, sir?

This time, what is it but despair in Eric's voice as he utters his *uh huh?*

Eric begins to suffer.

Maria is very disappointed.

She has moved back from the table and now she sits almost sideways in her chair: her legs crossed away from Eric, her body averted. She sips her wine, then holds the glass in her lap. When she looks down her hair swings over her face, hiding her profile.

She looks down now, frowning at her wine.

Eric is very disappointed.

The 'Boeuf Bordelaise' lacked garlic, among other things —notably *boeuf* — and was really a kind of non-commital stew. Placing his knife and fork in the position that means it's finished, he now sets aside the plate and turns to the waiting trifle. He dips his spoon into the cream, moves it around a little, then leans towards Maria and pleads with the hair:

At least I've been honest with you.

Maria looks up, but not at Eric. Her glance goes to the Ideal Couple, who are now beginning their steaks. Their conversation, less punctuated now by laughter, has obviously moved on to deeper, more serious topics. The young lady listens intently to what her escort is saying; the young man appears both elegant and sincere as he talks, and from his gestures alone it is possible to assume that he is well beyond all petty considerations and is already drawing analogies, guiding the discourse to its proper and highly interesting conclusion.

Maria drains her glass and puts it down in her lap. She looks down, hides behind her hair.

Maria, this is ridiculous.

This time she does glance at Eric, but it is over her shoulder virtually, and her eyes lack interest. She raises her eyebrows slightly:

Mmm?

When Eric throws his hands out to either side of his pudding, expressing his exasperation, his left wrist collides with the bottle. He watches in wonder as the wine blooms huge in the white linen, a beautiful blood-flower. His hand, acting on its own initiative, rights the bottle before it rolls off the edge of the table.

Christ I'll order another.

He pours the remaining inch of wine into his glass, then leans over the chair-back and waves the empty bottle at the waiter, the waiter who isn't there. He turns back to confront Maria, missing the table with his elbow.

I mean the way you're sitting Maria. How can I talk to your profile?

Reluctantly then Maria turns to face him, moves the chair forward a little, puts her glass on the table and begins to unwrap the frigid little triangle of camembert which turned out to be the fromage.

Eric, we can't afford another bottle.

Dejectedly she collects the dirty plates and cutlery, then lays them on top of the wide red stain on the tablecloth. It covers some of it, at least. She puts her elbows on the table, hiccups, presses her fingers into the roots of her hair, whispers:

Eric, don't you love me any more?

Eric brings his glass down on top of the little glass ashtray. The glass against the glass makes an unfortunate noise, and the Ideal Couple turn to stare in unison. Eric tries an apologetic smile. They look away pointedly, resuming their togetherness. Eric plays with his trifle and frowns as he considers this new riddle.

I think so . . . yes.

A barely perceptible quiver passes over Maria's lips and chin. Then a deeper tremor makes her cheeks shudder and her eyes close tightly. She raises her glass, holds it there, just a little below her chin. Evidently the glass is empty.

Maria, of course I . . .

But of course it is far too late: already she has bowed her head as the tears come, darting quickly from her eyes, racing one another down the cheeks, dripping from the curve of the chin. Grey spots occur here and there on the tablecloth as Maria, discreetly, weeps.

Eric offers her — oddly enough, still intact — his little paper boat.

Of course I do.

He looks around to see who's looking. No one seems to have noticed, and it is with a feeling of gratitude for this that Eric sends his hand over the table to pat Maria's bare arm. Of course he does, if the question should arise, love her.

Maria sniffs, hiccups, dabs her cheek with the crumpled boat, then sits up and bravely pushes the hair back from her face. Seeing the waiter approach, she excuses herself from the table.

Coffee, sir?

Eric nods but does not smile. As the waiter collects the dirty plates, Eric stutters an apology for the Red Sea underneath. The waiter makes a polite comment to the effect that it is nothing, then departs. Unwilling to face his schizoid twin in the alcove, Eric goes to the gents.

Maria has lost her self-respect.

Standing before the wash-hand basin, she searches for it in her bag. She finds a hairbrush, her mascara and the rectangular little mirror which, though too small for the job, presents her with a less literal self-portrait than the one she sees behind the taps. Even so she can see quite clearly that her eyelids are red-rimmed and swollen and that the mascara has trailed down her cheeks. Wondering if she is still attractive, Maria stoops to the running water and cups it in her hands. After splashing her face in it, she starts work on the disguise.

Eric has lost his self-respect.

Washing his hands, he searches for it in the mirror. He tries on various expressions, eyes his image from a number of angles. He attempts a broad, confident grin and his image leers back at him quickly. Sincerity comes next, and this time Eric has to avert his eyes. He tries on a few ugly faces: grotesque, gargoyle-like pouts; cross-eyed consternations; a doleful Frankenstein mask; demonic, wicked grins. Drying his fingers on a paper towel, he wonders if he is still an upright citizen. He zips up his flies.

Out in the restaurant, meanwhile, everything has been going on smoothly until now. The waiter has taken the opportunity, during Eric-and-Maria's absence, to clear up the debris they have strewn all over the table. Already he has delivered the coffee and the bill. But now, suddenly, something dreadful is happening at the next table. The young man, his fork on the way to his mouth, can hardly believe that it is really happening . . . but yes, it really is: she has stood up so abruptly that the chair has overturned. From her accent and appearance it is clear to everyone in the restaurant that she is a well brought-up, well educated girl but . . . . all that has gone, suddenly, and she is banging her fist hard on the table, making the dishes and the plates jump, and she is shouting, really shouting at the young man:

Bastard! You fucking . . . swine!

A unanimous silence. Then, perhaps because the swearwords were so well pronounced, a snigger. Then a gasp from another table, and a low-toned comment from another. The young lady, having burst loudly into tears, refuses to be pacified by either the waiter or the bastard-fucking-swine. Another waiter appears with the coats, and it is clear that the young man is being requested to leave — after settling his bill, of course. The young man says something quiet and earnest to the young lady as he takes out his wallet, but she won't wait another moment: breaking free of the many hands which seek to hold her and subdue her, she grabs her coat and her bag and marches adamantly out. The bastard-fucking-swine pays the bill, leaving a generous tip, and follows her — feeling the eyes on his back, sensing the theories being put forward at the tables around him.

It all happens so quickly that Eric and Maria, returning to their table from the toilets, are unaware that anything has happened. Indeed, they are mystified by the waiter's apology. But gradually, noticing that the next table has been hastily cleared, and sensing the scandalised chatter going on all around, they are able to surmise that something out of the ordinary has taken place at the next table in their absence. What it was, exactly, they can't imagine.

Eric takes out his cheque-book, turns the bill over and looks for the name of the restaurant. Underneath the name he notices a brief italicised message: *We hope you have enjoyed your meal. If you have, please come again soon, and tell all your friends about it!* And as he writes out the cheque Eric yawns repeatedly, and between the yawns there are fragments of a question:

Want to . . . go to . . . my place . . . or yours?

Maria's lips turn down at the corners with sincere disgust. She stirs the skin into her coffee, rattling the spoon in the cup.

Or how about both, Eric?

Eric looks up from his half-made signature, puzzled for a moment. Then, realising what Maria means, he proceeds with the surname. As the waiter collects the bill, Maria adds:

Or maybe you should call on Lillian?

Eric shakes his head, shrugs his shoulders and attempts a smile, uneasy that such a suggestion should have been made and impatient to leave the restaurant. And now that the meal is finished, and now that the bill has been paid, though Eric and Maria may yet have much to discuss, there is really nothing left to do but leave. And clearly they will have to go somewhere.

A Breakdown

PETEY YAWNED and watched the machine pick up another batch of tin cans, rotate, then put them down on the chute. They fell between one another as they rolled away, until they were rolling in single file, then disappeared through a narrow hole in the wall. On the other side of the wall, a mechanical finger would turn them upright and prod them on to a conveyor belt, which took them then to be filled, sealed and labelled. Before one batch had rolled away, the can-loading machine had picked up another in its rotating claw, and was already holding it in position above the chute. Petey blinked his eyes and yawned again. You had to admit it, that machine was fast. It could do the work of two men, and as Wilson, the production manager, had said the day it was installed, it *never* had to go to the toilet. He'd looked at Petey and Bill with that chilling look of his and added: it doesn't smoke. After that Bill had been put on inspection at the other end of the line, and now Petey's job was to operate the can-loading machine, which amounted to switching it off and on, and to watch out for damaged cans. If a bent can got into the sealing machine it could cause it to jam, then the whole line would be held up.

Petey rubbed his eyes with his knuckles. It wasn't so easy to do nothing after all, and the noise of the machine and the endless watching had given him a dull pain behind the eyes. He'd had headaches at work before, but this was a different kind of pain: dull, persistent. He'd had it for a few days now, just behind the eyes. He'd have preferred a real headache to this not-quite-a-headache which never seemed to go away completely. Sometimes he thought it wasn't a pain at all, that it was all in the mind, but then he would feel it again: dull, a feeling of deadness, as if something had seized up. Before the machine had been installed, he'd found the work hard on the back — he was an old man, after all —but at least he'd had Bill to talk to. Now the only people he saw were Wilson, who came round to check up on him every so often, and the fork-lift driver every time he brought round a new stack of cans. But neither of these men were willing to stop and have a bit of a conversation. That's what happened to you when you got old: you weren't worth talking to any more, your words didn't count.

Petey got down off the stool and walked over to the stack of empty cans. Each stack had a dozen layers, and between each layer there was a sheet of card. Petey had to discard the card, so that the machine could move on to the next layer. He waited until it had picked up the last batch of cans, and when he pulled away the card the silver rims of the next layer gleamed like a steel honeycomb. He picked out one of the shining cells and looked at his elongated reflection in its surface. Like a face on T.V. when the vertical hold has gone . . . or was it the horizontal hold? One of the holds, anyway. Petey squeezed the tin between the palms of his hands, until he felt it give and crumple. When he looked at himself again, part of his face was missing. He walked around the chute and watched them rolling down: they seemed to be grinning at him, like a row of teeth. He took the one he'd crushed, a bad tooth, and slipped it between the others. It didn't roll too well, but the momentum of the others carried it down until it disappeared through the hole in the wall.

Wilson came around the wall and swiped the air with his hand, meaning cut the power. Other people would've tried to shout above the noise of the machine, but not Wilson. Petey pushed the STOP button and a red light showed. The machine stopped, a clutch of hollow cans held high above the stack. In the sudden silence there was the rapid click of Wilson's heels as he approached. Something about that sound made Petey want to shiver. The way the man looked at you too, and talked to you, it was eerie.

'There's been a breakdown,' said Wilson.

'What?'

'The line has been held up. You may take a break.'

'Is the line held up?'

'Yes.'

'Can I go to the canteen?'

Wilson smiled. It was a patient little smile, the kind of smile you might use with a child who asks for something he can't have.

'I'm afraid it isn't open yet.'

Petey appeared to think this over, conscious of Wilson's even gaze on him. You couldn't look at the eyes like that, you had to let them look at you. Why didn't the man say something?

'What's up anyway?' said Petey.

'The sealing machine is jammed. We think a damaged can —'

'I didn't see any,' Petey declared, averting his eyes. After a long moment of silence, Wilson turned and went back around the wall. The efficient click of those heels. When he was gone, Petey got down off the stool and began stamping some life into his feet. He leaned his elbow on the stool and looked at the control box: apart from the STOP button with the red light, there was the GO button with the green light and, underneath them, a black switch with the word PAUSE printed above it. Below that there was the dial which set the speed. For a moment it looked like a rudimentary face, with two different coloured eyes and an open mouth. Petey smiled and shook his head, then he felt it again, that dead feeling. He took out his tobacco and his matches, then furtively rolled a thin cigarette between his fingers.

'Hear that?' said Petey to the machine, ' "There has been a breakdown. You may take a break"!' He smiled to himself. It was four in the morning, the line was held up and here he was, the saboteur: an old man with a pain in the head, talking to a machine. 'I must be going crazy,' he said, then put the cigarette between his lips and struck a match. He found himself blinking, startled, when the flame appeared, as if it were the last thing he expected. As he smoked he rolled another cigarette, and he noticed that his hands were trembling. Sometimes they did shake a little, but not as badly as this — as if something had given him a bad fright. 'Maybe I *am* going crazy,' he said, laying the badly-rolled cigarette on top of the control box. He saw the face again, laughed a little and said: 'That one's for you.' He chuckled at the idea of it — a man talking to a machine — but still, it was better than not talking at all. 'Go on,' he said to it, 'have a smoke before Wilson comes back.' After a moment he added: 'Course, I forgot. You don't smoke, do you?'

He looked behind him to see if anyone was around. If someone heard him offering the machine a cigarette ... 'They'd think I was talking to myself,' said Petey to the machine, 'but I'll tell you something: I may be old, but I'm not senile. I just ... think aloud sometimes. It's different.' The machine, as if attempting a rejoinder, let fall one of the cans from its hooked and gleaming fingers. It fell on top of the stack, and the tin against the tin made an argumentative noise. Petey was startled by the noise, then he laughed. He walked over to the stack and picked up the fallen can, then came back and dangled it in front of the red and green eyes. 'You dropped one,' said Petey, 'you're not so hot.' He chuckled a little as he walked back to the stack, shaking his head from side to side and repeating, 'You're not so hot.' The honeycomb pattern made by the shining rims spun around suddenly, and the inside of one can seemed to swell up, as if a tin had decided to open its mouth and speak. But it didn't want to speak, it wanted to eat. Petey felt himself falling into the shining mouth, but he stopped himself in time, putting a hand in front of his eyes.

'Jesus, what's wrong with me tonight?' said Petey, squinting up to where the claw of the machine waited above the stack. He backed away, climbed up on the stool, then lit the second cigarette. His hands were shaking badly now, and as he looked around him his lips were moving slightly, as if he were trying to recall something, a word or a phrase which would let him know where he was and what he was meant to do there.

'Maybe you are fast,' he said, 'but listen, if you work your guts out one night, they expect it of you the next. And the next, and every night. You wouldn't catch me and Bill . . . we went at our own pace. Sent a man round, a work-study man. Listen, what we did was . . . we picked up eight, eight at a time, instead of . . . .' Petey held out his hands and spread the fingers. You could get one on each finger and trap another two between the handfuls. '. . . instead of twelve, how about that? Said we were as fast as what was it . . . humanly possible.' He went on, his voice growing quiet, speaking absently to the machine: 'It's okay for you, you never had a childhood . . . you don't know what it's like to . . . *play*.' The word sounded odd as he said it, slightly ridiculous. He repeated it a few times, quietly, to himself, until he no longer knew what it meant. He thought of the playground at the school he'd gone to so many years ago, with its tall iron railings and the windowless shelter for when it rained. He could see them all, as if from above, all the children playing in the playground, but none of them had a face, and what were they playing at?

Petey shook his head and rubbed his eyes with his knuckles. When he looked up he saw the row of cans on the steel chute, waiting to roll away. They looked like teeth, bared in a grin. When they came towards him and made to bite, Petey jumped down from the stool and, shuddering violently, held out a warning finger and began uttering threats and curses in a voice that wasn't like his voice. But suddenly he was aware that he was standing there and threatening what was, after all, only a row of tin cans on a chute. As he lowered his arm and looked up at the claw of the machine and saw that it was just a mechanical device for picking up cans . . . and how could a few buttons on a control box resemble a face? Petey pressed his temples with his hands. 'Take a walk,' he said quietly, 'you need to get out, get some air.'

Wilson pushed open the rubber flap of the factory door and saw the huddled figure by the factory wall.

'There you are.'

'Yes, I'm here.'

'I've been all over the factory, looking for you.'

'I thought I'd get a breath of air.'

'The line's been going for almost an hour.'

'Listen, is it playtime yet?'

'Pardon?'

'Is it playtime? Don't get me wrong, I've worked all my life, I'm a good worker, but that machine tried to attack me. I had to come out into the playground, but nobody else came out. I didn't see any, on my oath. You wouldn't catch me and Bill. Mister Wilson, is it playtime yet?'

Wilson took the old man's arm and began to guide him towards the door.

'Yes,' he said, 'it's playtime now.'

The Sky

IT IS TUESDAY so I go to see Doctor Pleasingham. It's my twentieth session, but do I progress? If anything I deteriorate. Sometimes I wish he would tell me. There is nothing I can do for you Paul, you're a hopeless case. Or if he'd told me the first time I went to him. To get out and not come back. Nothing much wrong with you I'm a busy man. Nothing a good night out won't cure. Nothing a good old episode of sexual intercourse won't.

He used that exact phrase. An episode of it, imagine. But if he'd told me then, maybe I'd have pulled myself together on the spot. Some hope. But the phrase is right because I've come apart. Like my copy of the A to Z, all the pages loose from the binding. All jumbled up in the wrong order, that's me. And some I fear are lost.

Impossible to find your way anywhere with it. And so it is with my pages. Painstaking Doctor Pleasingham is trying to find his way to me. Impossible. To find out which parts join up with which. And which are missing. Each district of my mind is right. But the order, the connections between. I would rather sit at home and watch the sky.

He is sitting on the edge of his desk when I go in. Half sitting, with his legs crossed at the ankles. Sometimes I go in and he's putting. He keeps a putter there in the consulting room. And a thing that serves as the hole. It returns the golfball to him. How tedious for him to listen all day to people's misery. He could be striding out there along the fairway. I could caddy for him, out there under the open sky. Think of the therapy involved. Teeing up Doctor Pleasingham's balls. But I fear we have landed in a bunker.

'Ah Paul how are you, had a good week?'

I hate this part when I'm standing with my coat on, before it starts. I want to walk out. Run right along the corridor and down the six flights of stairs. I have the idea that something sudden might shake me out of it. Jolt me out of this into life again. I would like to believe in sudden and beautiful things. A miracle that changes everything.

'So-so doctor you know how it is. The weather hasn't been too good. Bit clearer today, but cold.'

Some sudden miracle making everything clear again and simple.

He smiles and comes away from his desk. He's pleased with this business about the weather. To his ears this is music. He's positively chuffed. He sees it as evidence I think. Of my return to life, to normality. I think sometimes for Doctor Pleasingham the one equals the other. Save me from that slow death as well as this one. Make it quick and clean and simple.

We stand for a moment not knowing what to say. Looking out the big glass window at the sky. There it is doctor, yet another evening on the planet Earth. Insects and helicopters buzzing round. Underground spewing out its millions. Every one of us, doctor, every one of us.

'Yes indeed somewhat chilly.'

So slow. So slow and methodical Doctor Pleasingham rubs his hands together. The knuckles of one in the palm of the other. Meaning indeed somewhat chilly, and let's get down to our business. I'm his last patient on a Tuesday. He wants to get home to play with his roses, prune his kids and have an episode of sexual intercourse. Poor old Doctor Pleasingham wants his little corner of the sky. Has to suffer mine instead. It's the highlight of my week. It is.

'Shall we take up our positions Paul?'

This with a touch of irony. Not a touch but an intonation. But it would touch me if I could be touched. I am touched, touched in the head. I hang up my coat on the coatstand. And we do take up our positions. He in the armchair by the window, me on the couch. Both of us aware of the cliche of it. As in all the best cartoons, but no matter. I can lie here and look at the sky.

'Now then Paul, you were telling me last week. In fact for the past few weeks now we've been mainly concerned with this ah . . . gap you feel. This gap you feel is growing, coming between you and ah . . . things.'

Takes off the hornrims. Breathes on them. Looks at me with a narrowing eye. Then down at what he's doing. Polishing the lenses with a handkerchief. A sunbeam slanting through the window there. His bald stark skull. Patch of well-cropped stubble there above each ear. Scalp weatherbeaten and browned from all those hours on the golf course. Like the skin of a basted fowl. This is part of the trouble isn't it. I don't see Doctor Pleasingham. I see the species. Myself also. The creatures we are, the little killers. His smile a baring of the teeth, mine too and I mean it. I have to make such efforts to believe. To believe in these words together. I hear more the intonation. Now then Paul.

'Now then Paul, if I were to ask you to choose one word, one word to sum up this feeling of the ah . . . gap, which word would you choose?'

I appear to think about it. Then I do think about it, then I lose it. He puts the glasses back on. Edges them up on the narrow bridge of his nose. Adjusts the legs behind his ears. He's trimmed his mustache. How simple to grow a mustache, and to trim it. He's only human as they say. This would move me if I could be moved. The gap. Which gap? This gap between me and Doctor Pleasingham. Between the words and the meaning. The sunlight flashing on his lenses like that.

'Dissociation doctor.'

He tilts his head back. The sky reflecting from his lenses. Between his eyes and mine the sky. So clear and simple and endless.

'Good Paul, very good.'

He likes my word. We've played this game before, this word game. Choose one word to sum up all the other words. Last time I said handicap. He didn't appreciate the pun.

'Could we begin with that word, Paul? The word itself isn't crucial, but we must begin with something, mustn't we?'

And end up with nothing. Nothing but the gap. Begin the twentieth session with a word game.

'Yes doctor.'

Settle down now and watch the sky. A clear sky, blue. Bit of a cloud out there above the university. I get the feeling sometimes he can read them. These thoughts that hurry in and out. Don't stop long enough to have time to. Time to think them out, I need time to . . . Time to time, these thoughts. This feeling he can sometimes.

Is he waiting for me or am I him? Who is waiting for whom? In any case, the gap. Sometimes I think neither does he. Know who is waiting for whom. Clearing his throat and looking through the big window at it there.

'So let's begin with the word you've chosen Paul, and work our way outwards from it shall we?'

Hands translating the outwards. Spreads the fingers. Moves them round an invisible ball. If a blind man at the beach. Were to pick up a beach ball. Now then Paul.

'Expand upon it and explain it as best you can. Take it slowly Paul, we're in no hurry. Add to it little by little, until we've built up a fairly complete picture of the problem.'

He pauses to look out at the sky. The softening light spreading out its fingers. If a blind man were to pick up the sun. Doctor Pleasingham picks up the sentence in his head. Think of it.

'Think of it as a picture Paul. You've begun by making a mark on the blank canvas. You don't know what the mark is going to be. Add to it a little at a time, then we'll see if some shape emerges. All right?'

'All right.'

And next week we'll colour it in. Why not leave it blank? Lie here and watch it spreading out. That light, that immaculate blue. One violet stripe of cloud. Well then Paul.

'Well then Paul, try to tell me what you mean by this ah . . . dissociation, hmm?'

'I just mean I don't feel . . . I mean what the word means. The feeling, no not the feeling. The idea, no not the idea. The fact of being apart from doctor. Not getting through to doctor. Having no contact with doctor. That's all I mean doctor.'

Leather elbow patches on the arms of the chair. Noting something down there. A note of dissociation. Now patting the chair with his hand.

I see the sky in his lenses, that long ribbon of cloud.

'Yes Paul, I do know the word and I think I'm familiar with its usage. I meant you to give me an example of this ah . . . dissociation you feel. No matter how trivial it may seem to you. Begin with one small example.'

No matter how trivial, of course. It will not be so trivial for Doctor Pleasingham. We all make fools of ourselves unwittingly. We give ourselves away every moment. Doctor Pleasingham will look at my example. Like a man watching the sunset for helicopters.

'Everything doctor. It's difficult.'

He knows I'm stalling. He likes it when I'm stalling. Thinks he's getting warm, thinks he's in the right area. Maybe he is, but the area's been demolished. Due for redevelopment soon. Paul I've come to the conclusion. What you need is a new identity. This is the national health range, these over there are a little more expensive. Well now.

'Well now, if everything is an example of it as you say, it shouldn't be so difficult to give me one example, now should it?'

'No doctor.'

It shouldn't, should it? To should or not to should, that's the question.

'But it is difficult doctor, I'm afraid I'm not being very helpful.'

He puts the pen in his top pocket. Clasps his hands over the notes. It means nothing is happening. Nothing worth noting. He'll stay like that now. Staring out into the endless.

'It's partly my memory doctor. I can't keep hold of the connection. Between this week and last week. Or now and a moment ago.'

Doctor Pleasingham resting the mustache on the clasped hands. Looks over the tops of the hornrims. He doesn't like it. This mention of memory. We've been through all this memory stuff before. It didn't get us anywhere. It's history now, forget it.

'Your memory, Paul, seems to be all right. You remember we conducted a series of tests. It isn't your memory we want to focus on now. It's more what you've called your dissociation. Let's get back to that, shall we?'

'Yes doctor. For example this. This is an example of dissociation. Lying here talking to you doctor. What I mean by dissociation. And what I mean by what I mean by it. If you follow me doctor. That's what it's like, two mirrors. Two mirrors reflecting each other. I step back from myself, and I step back again. Until I'm far away from myself. Not only myself. Everything.'

I can tell he's keen on the mirrors. He's taken out his pen again. Making a note of those mirrors there.

'Could we take this a little more slowly Paul? One thing at a time.'

Doctor Pleasingham wants to take it more slowly. Of course we can take it more slowly. Go right back to the beginning and start all over again. Or grind to a halt here and now. I'll go home and hang the word dissociation above the fire. Stare at it. Now then Paul.

'Now then Paul, you say this is an example of dissociation, this situation you are in now. Could you explain what it feels like?'

'Locked up doctor. I can't get out of myself. Can't get myself out. I'm rotting inside. Sometimes I think I can smell it. Like a corpse doctor in a cupboard. Because I don't . . . engage. Not only with you doctor and other people. But with myself. And with things, objects. Because of the . . . gap.'

'How does this feeling of being ah . . . trapped, locked up, begin Paul? This feeling of the gap, the dissociation?'

Doctor Pleasingham loves that word of mine. He's going to use it in the golf club. I became rather dissociated from the game around the eleventh hole. Tried using a four iron but couldn't get out of the bunker. I couldn't engage with the ball. How does it start? This is how it starts, it starts here.

'I get up in the morning doctor. And someone who needs a shave looks out at me from the mirror. Then it starts . . . the gap.'

He pushes the hornrims back up on his nose. They've slipped. He's been writing. Writing down that corpse in the cupboard alongside the two mirrors. Maybe he'll quote my case in a learned paper. A classic case of chronic dissociation, curable only by a sudden miracle. Go on Paul.

'Go on Paul, go on. Let's have a few other examples.'

Doctor Pleasingham the blind man asking me what red is. I say, for example an apple. For example, a sunset. For example blood, a telephone box, the cross on the ambulance doors. I go on giving examples. But having no experience of colour, he still can't say what red means.

'For example pain.'

That sky out there and here we are on the sixth floor with pain. It's the gap that really hurts.

'I mean my own pain doctor. I call it mine. I tell myself it's my own. To own my pain and make it mine doctor. To engage with it. To be part of that if nothing else. But even then . . . the gap. I feel it all right, I feel pain. But it passes through me doctor like a train.'

'A train?'

'A train through a station. It doesn't stop, none do. The station's been closed down, it's deserted. The weeds are everywhere. The ticket office all boarded up. In the waiting room, dirty drawings. A bad smell. These thoughts that hurry . . . don't stop. They don't stop long enough to . . . I'm sorry doctor, could you remind me of the point?'

Writing furiously away there. Noting down that disused station with the corpse in the cupboard and the mirrors. A classic case.

'Dissociation Paul.'

'O yes. Dissociation doctor.'

'The gap you feel between . . .'

'Between myself and . . .'

Doctor Pleasingham scratching his mustache with the pen. He's waiting for me. But I've given him enough to go on with. Enough examples of red. Now he has to see it for himself. Rather lie here and watch the sky. To be out there, part of that emptiness. Part of that endless clear and simple. Now Paul.

'Now Paul, that's good. Would you mind now telling me again about the first time you experienced this ah . . . dissociation from the world, and from yourself?'

'But it wasn't like that doctor. It was gradual. It happened to me without my knowing it had happened. I realised I'd been apart from everything, not connecting with anything, out of the world, for a long time. I don't know when it started. I think maybe at birth.'

Doctor Pleasingham's lenses flashed in the light. He moved a little. Only a little. But quickly. I surprised him.

'You can't remember a time when you haven't felt this Paul?'

'No doctor.'

Note that down there under the deserted station. Still it won't stop the trains. The trains of my thought. I hear them coming then they're gone. But I was under.

'But I was under the impression, Paul, that you first experienced this . . . gap, one day on a picnic with friends.'

He wants the story of the picnic before he goes home. How may times do I have to tell him it? He should know it by heart by now. But he's slow. Lacks imagination. That's why he likes the story of the picnic. It makes everything clear to him and simple. But everything isn't clear, everything isn't simple.

'Isn't that so, Paul?'

'No doctor. That was the first time I . . . discovered the gap. It had been there all along. But I hadn't noticed it. Hadn't realised it. If you can imagine a painter doctor. He's been painting pictures all his life. One day he has eye strain. He goes to the optician. The optician tests his eyes. It turns out that as well as having strained eyes, he's colourblind. He sees red instead of green, green instead of red. The painter goes home and looks at his pictures. Realises they're all wrong.'

'Yes Paul, I understand what you're saying.'

He understands it but it makes no difference. Doctor Pleasingham the colourblind painter hasn't had eye-strain yet. Hasn't suffered the realisation. That there are some diseases you must catch. Must contract before you can cure. If he really put himself in my place. It would spoil his golf. Ruin his handicap.

'But let's focus on the moment when you became aware, became conscious of the fact that you were . . . dissociated.'

Doctor Pleasingham going through his motions. I mine. The difference is only this. That I am conscious that they are the motions. Whereas he . . . he has not fallen into it. Has not come across . . . the gap. Perhaps if I grew a mustache. Trimmed it assiduously. Begin by believing in your mustache. Work your way outwards from it. Do you think.

'Do you think, Paul, you could tell me again exactly what happened on that day of the picnic?'

'Yes doctor.'

This is part of the trouble, isn't it? I start talking to Doctor Pleasingham. It's difficult, but I start. I play along. I think of a word. I add another word and another. It gets easier. Easier to talk like this. He sees it as progress. What he can't see is the gap. Between me and what I say, the gap. He can't see that the more I appear to be involved, the less I'm involved. He's never felt the gap.

'It was a Saturday doctor.'

To hear my own voice talking like this. Pathetic. Like a man with a stutter. Trying desperately to tell someone. That he has a stutter. Go on Paul.

'Go on Paul.'

'Julie and Graham, friends of Martha's. Suggested we went for a picnic. In Graham's car. It was a good day for it doctor. Sunny. We bought wine. Martha made some food. Chicken legs, fruit, bread and cheese.'

I always put in that bit about the chicken legs. There were no chicken legs. But I have to take Doctor Pleasingham on this picnic with me. He might as well enjoy some chicken legs. His imagination needs. Something to bite on. He's waiting for the rest of the story.

'We drove out to the hills. Weather was perfect. So we drank the wine doctor, ate the food. I told that joke doctor, that joke about Adam and Eve and the snake. You want me to go over it again doctor?'

'No Paul, just what happened.'

'Well, we played one or two games doctor. We were drunk you understand. We played kid's games, and one of the games was catch-kiss.'

Doctor Pleasingham nods. He can't wait for the bit about the sky.

'And I think it was Martha who was chasing me. The whole things sounds silly doctor. I fell down . . . a gap. I didn't hurt myself doctor. But when I landed I was on my back and . . . and then it happened. The sky. The sky came down and came into me. It felt like that. Or that I'd soared out of myself to meet the sky.'

This is the moment he wants me to relive. Instead he relives it. I merely tell him the story. One day perhaps at this moment in the story, he'll look out at the sky. And it will come into him. Or he will go up to meet it. Until then . . . the gap. That's all.

'That's all, Paul?'

'The sky had come into me doctor. It was a part of me and I was a part of it. They laughed at me. Then thought I had concussion. That's when I first became conscious of . . . the gap, the dissociation. But it had always been there doctor.'

'But you'd never felt it before this ah . . . fall?'

'No doctor.'

Doctor Pleasingham looking out there at it all. All of it. But seeing only his little corner of it. His little corner of normality. His little corner of the sky.

'Good Paul. Each time you tell the ah . . . story of the picnic, you remember it a little more clearly, I think. Soon we may be able to tell exactly why this event ah . . . took place as it did.'

'You think I'm making progress doctor?'

There I am asking that question, but really I am looking out at the sky. To be out there again, to be part of it.

'Yes indeed Paul. Soon I think you may be able to resume your studies.'

Doctor Pleasingham thinks this is important. That I should resume my studies. Show me how to resume my life. Looking out at the red gold glow of it above the university there. Now Paul.

'Now Paul, prior to this event, can you remember if you were suffering from ah . . .'

Stress of any kind. But I've given up on the session. This one and every one. The gap will always be there. It always has been. I cannot go back to my childhood. In the same way I cannot go back to before that moment when the sky . . . Doctor Pleasingham wants me to go back. Wants me to resume where I left off. I can't. I have to learn to live with . . . the gap. I hear my voice telling him about sleep.

'And does anything else, apart from sleep, give you relief from this feeling of dissociation?'

'Only when I look at the sky.'

Doctor Pleasingham gets tired of me and the sky. I don't blame him. And when he suggests that he pulls the blinds, I agree. Less distraction from the words. The words go on and on without us, and we never meet. If I caddied for him it would be better. By the time we get to my childhood again it's the end of the session. Continue next week where we left it. Except that I won't be here. It shouldn't make much difference. I'm not here anyway. Doctor Pleasingham taking off his glasses. Rubbing his tired old eyes. Poor old colourblind painter. I put on my coat. While my back is turned he zips up the blinds. What's he up to, shock therapy? It's quite something.

'It's quite something tonight, isn't it Paul?'

I turn around and there he is, the species. Hand held out to it. The panoramic view.

'What doctor?'

He smiles. His mustache spreading out like the night.

'The sky, Paul, the sky.'

I go for the door.

'Oh that. Yes quite something. Tonight and every night.'

Jinglebells

Jesuschristalmighty what a hellhole.

Morning I mean, I mean afternoon. Night morelike anyway, nearly dark already for christsake and here we are just out of the hay as usual. Xmas day no different from any other suffering day except. Except nothing. We are awake, the least said the better. Whence this royal plural all of a sudden I would like to know. The delusions of grandeur intact and still going strong apparently. Room in the same unholy bloody execrable mess as usual I see. Mess is the word. Last night I dreamt that I stood on a freshly laid wad of dogshit, burnt sienna in colour and still warm and steaming from the bodyheat of its creator. Look up Freud under symbols dogshit. Begin.

Who am I?

On christmas morn I mean night, after tea and cigarettes as usual, you resolve to make a fresh start a slate clean and this is what you come up with. Who am I? I am an identity crisis with a bad hangover in need of a way to begin. Begin what I would like to know. One has to make a start somewhere however. However messy. But what was it Picasso I think it was said about having to get back to it before you can start from it. Scratch I mean. If only I knew what the scratch was I could maybe get back there and start from it. Get a grip of yourself man before it's too late, the year is drawing to a close and what do you have to show for it? Next to nothing, if that. Yet the situation is urgent and will continue to be so until. Until what I would like to know? Until you take yourself in hand and. On second thoughts, but to begin.

I am an aspiring

expiring morelike painter. Of no specific school, unless you count

119

the redbrick building whose greyhaired guardians had the foresight to expel me at a tender age into the world of adult unemployment. Presently between positions then, though I have been known to work on a casual temporary part time basis in the subterranean kitchens of a hamburger restaurant. Also steaks salads milkshakes of all flavours together with blueberry cheesecake and frenchfries. The menu would make one puke. Where I perform certain necessary rites alongside one lyric poet of my aquaintance and the other addicts. That cook is the worst, throwing eggs at the radio and the hamburgers all over the shop, temperamental does not express it. Psychotic more like the way he hacks the steaks off with that cleaver all the time cursing his luck and drinking from an unlabelled bottle a clear liquid he calls whisky. And the black gobbets of grease dripping from the overhead pipes into your hair, all that foetid meat hanging from hooks dripping blood into the pancake batter and the bare bulb dangling over the garbage sack. You'd think electricity had just been invented for crying out loud. All the orders being stuck on the spike and the sinks blocking up and the radio going bananas, it's a worse hellhole than this and that's saying something. On the other hand, what? On the other hand this work, though unseemly and poorly paid, may be looked upon as research of a kind, Orwellian in nature, which doubtless will provide you with the raw material for a series of large scale compositions at a later date. You cannot deny either that it gets you out of the house, and then there is always the hamburger at the end of the night to consider. Food, when all is said and done. Is more important than art.

Listen to it.

There is yet a certain dignity in your position. One disdains to become the prostitute of the gallery world and the media. Not that opportunities come thick and fast, however. However you are even now the proud possessor of one paintspattered college property easel, a bag of massacred oils and — there is hope for the century yet — a stretched and sized canvas awaiting desecration. In the final analysis then I am more than ever in a position to begin. May well be on the verge of a breakthrough. The first brushstroke will tell all. Presently the equipment mentioned stands by the window, where it serves as both coatstand and screen, this window being curtainless due to a recent accident of no moment. It happened last night. After my six hour slog in the aforesaid dungeon, followed by a drunken celebration of the eve of it all on the way home to this. This my ill-furnished solitude of dogshit nightmares.

I am a hamburger of no moment.

Personally I don't see how you intend to begin anything or get back to anything with the possible exception of bed. Get back in there among the dying embers of your bodyheat man, before it's too late. Cooling already probably. In any event, it resembles too much the lair of a reptile to be tempting. Not that I'm any authority on the subject of reptile lairs if they sleep in lairs. And I don't see why they shouldn't given that I have to. No, not have to. Choose to. Always a one for splitting the hair. In any event I cannot get back under those scratchy blankets after such a comparison. On the other hand, sleep. During sleep at least the mind falls briefly into disuse, except they plague you with dogturd symbols even then. Who is this they you are talking about I would like to know? I shall not get back into bed, on the grounds that it is unpleasantly odorous. Why the unpleasantly, one is only human? Why the one when it's at home, and for that matter why the only?

I am only human.

In any event I cannot continue. But to resume, cannot continue this life of unsocial hours. Retiring shortly before dawn, rising shortly before nightfall. No way of life for an aspiring man of your age and outlook. Outlook listen to it, who do you think you are Bertrand Russell or what. And you have the temerity to call this a way of life, why not say lifestyle and be hanged. For a sheep as a lamb as they say. There they are again, the same crowd you blame for your dreams. As if I could afford a lifestyle. The mess this place is in, think what your Auntie Mary would say. Ah kent he wis a bad bugger the minute Ah clapped eyes on him. Too late even to nip round the corner and enter into small but meaningful business transactions with butcher baker and newsagent. The three wise men, anyway they're shut remember it being the day of our etcetera. A paper would be the thing. Refresh your abhorrence of current events. Have a read at the problems corner for a laugh.

121

You heartless bastard you should be writing in there yourself for some good solid advice. Dear Mrs Earhole, my problem is I don't know where to begin don't think I can go on and dread to think where it will all end, yours desperate.
P.S. my dreams have disturbing canine-scatological implications is this normal for an unmarried man. Dear desperate your problem is that you have too much time weighing heavy on your hands why not put them to good use and get a job in a hamburger restaurant dishwashing, yours Earhole. P.S. why not donate your dreams to your nearest Jungian research unit.

Give us a break.

But who was it said what was it. Modern man fornicates and reads the newspapers, Albert Camus probably. Hesitate to quote seeing as it took me long enough to pronounce his name right. I recall trying to chat up a girl in our first year, new out of a girl's convent and fresh as an early Matisse. On second thoughts make it a daisy. So there I am telling the whole miserable story of l'etranger, all about this bloke who goes out and tops a complete stranger for no reason and so forth. Needless to say doing my worst to impress her with a few of my first big words like exist-stench-all. All this taking place in the customary bedsit of the time you understand, with the gas meter on the fire there and one or two symbolic paint stains on the lino. Me hoping doubtless that this was all in the nature of a bedtime story and would inspire her to random acts of uninhibited carnality. Her sitting there on the bed edge listening seriously and nodding all the way through the thing until the denouement if it had one. Then she says it sounds familiar I may have read it but who is the author. And I tell her it's by Albert, as in Tatlock, Came-us. Then she thinks for a minute and says O! You mean kah-moo! And there was me thinking he was probably from Yorkshire. The humiliations I have suffered at the hands of female oppressors.

I am modern man.

Mind you I can't say I do much these days in the way of fornication or the papers. The really committed modern man of course does both at once while watching the telly. Xmas is therefore a problem for poor old modern man. No paper to read for christsake. Which leaves one with fornication. If only I had somebody to fornicate with, but no. No hope of any such intercourse. If only I could qualify as a miserable sinner, I could subscribe with a clear conscience to what's it called, the Watchtower. Who knows, I may have visitors yet. A pair of christians sent round the doors of the ill and infirm, bearing leaflets of comfort and joy. The thing is ladies I am in the middle of my preprandial selfabuse at the moment, could you come back tomorrow or the dayafter? Or perhaps a group of carolsinging girlguides will station themselves beneath my window to bring a note of cheer. Not content with exposing himself indecently, the accused then proceeded to urinate from his firstfloor window upon the heads of these innocent christians.

It has the indecency to snow.

I worked up the courage to go to the window and look out at the world, fired by my imaginary girlguides I have no doubt. And by christ it's a white one all right, blowing a thick bloody blizzard out there and no mistake. Visibility nil. Deaths will result I am certain. Not a sign of life in the cul-de-sac, not a jinglebell. Not even a solitary suffering light on except mine, where is everybody at church or what. Maybe they've all perished except me. Divine retribution doubtless. Doubtless I deserve it. This life of solitary farting and scratchy blankets. I recall the last time I strongarmed a friend into sharing that hellish little mattress with me in a night of erotic abandon. She complained next morning of a rash upon her neck, whereupon I was not slow to point out that this was by no means the worst place to have developed such a rash after such a night and she should count her blessings.

As if hygiene were paramount.

Admittedly I have not washed shaved or groomed my person for several days. Therefore smell powerfully of hamburger, not to mention the more intimate odours. But this is all to the good as I see it. As I see it, the day will dawn soon — the first of the new year perhaps it's as well to get tradition behind you — and I shall rise again. But this time at a predetermined hour, having set the clock etcetera. Yawn stretch and so forth. Congratulate oneself on a sound night's kip and the fecundity of one's subconcious.

Confront then the matted and grizzled being in the mirror and exclaim, *This has gone far enough*. Then, think of it, the untrammelled orgy of ablution. He emerges from the bathroom a pure being, cleansed not only of the facial weed and the greaseclots from the pipes and the more personal bodily grimes, but also of all doubt all misgiving. All spiritual filth scrubbed away, the mind a canvas perfectly blank. Back at scratch at last. A clean shirt can do wonders for a man in my position. They defer naturally to the integrity of freshly ironed trousers, the humility of wellworn but polished shoes. There they are again, you're obsessed with this they.

I am what I think they think I am.

A cleansed spirit, I shall then fulfil without ostentation my duties as a spiritual teacher. Pass on the simple wisdom which has come to me over the years of contemplation kitchen work and infrequent washing. The fundamental solution to modern man's moral predicament when faced with the senseless hurlyburly of the modern world. Perhaps agree to publish these teachings, the text a literary and philosophical masterpiece translated into eighty-eight languages with far reaching implications for mankind. Illustrated of course by the author. Either that or they'd take you for a moron. Hapless idiot, you can tell it's his mum washes and dresses him just by looking at him, and him in his thirties. Institutions for the likes of him where he can do something useful with his time, occupational therapy say. Making aluminium bottletops all day while waiting for christmas to come round with a visit from Leslie Crowther if he's lucky. Them again, who is this they you have in mind tell me straight? Crowd of bastards by the sound of it.

I think they think I am what I am not.

Well they're wrong whoever the hell they are. Still a wash might be a step in the right direction, back to scratch as Picasso said. But who else was it said my advice to painters is improve on the blank canvas, Kruschev probably. And where is the integrity in a life dedicated to the corruption of the human spirit? I mean the mess you make of everything. Room like a bomb's hit it okay. Maybe burglars. Easygoing sorts just doing a spot of breaking-and on the way home from the pub, probably whistling mares-eat-oats-and-does-eat-oats-and-little-lambs-eat-ivy as they jemmy open the door and start in on the drawers. Good honest burglars the likes of which have only been known in the pages of the Beano ever since they rolled back a boulder and found an empty ditch. Here somebody's pinched the Messiah. The state of this place would certainly give your Auntie Mary a coronary on the spot. All these drawers hanging out at all angles, like steps in a stairwell. All that drivel spilling out of them, your garments I suppose. All those dogeared plates and halfeaten books on the floor, I tell you the situation deteriorates daily. And what about that shirt on the chairback there, it makes me want to weep the way it's lying there. Arms bent wrongwise at the elbows like a man drowning for pity's sake. There's a metaphor here complete with capsized curtains the lot if you're not careful, me in the crow's nest screaming land ahoy as we go under.

How futile.

On a more sober note the narrator would like to point out that certainly it looks very much as if. As if violence has taken place upon these premises in the recent past. A dim recollection of returning to the abode in a condition of drunken grandeur. Whereupon followed certain acts of violence, meaningless in themselves but performed with an air of conviction, upon the inanimate furnishings and fittings. Hence the capsized curtains, flotsam of books plates etcetera. Often I believe I am a grievous bodily harm man myself, not the aggressor of course but a willing victim. Something inside one calls out to be lacerated. But who was it said that . . . It was that famous expressionist I met while holidaying in Wales. There you are you see, holidaying. Can't say I remember his name right off, everybody said he was too much in the shadow of somebody else whose name I can't remember either. So there I am holidaying with my cycling partner of the time in the Welsh mountainsides. You see how jolly idealistic one was in those days and now look at you. And anyway this famous expressionist offers us lodgings in his Welsh cottage there for a night or two. Don't ask me why, maybe he liked having a couple of cyclists about the house to impart a bit of his expressionism to by the fire. Anyway one morning he says to me he says, Do you believe there is such a thing as a rape-ee? This over the tea and toast you understand in the middle of nowhere in Wales. Well I says, you could try advertising for one.

The temptations of anecdote.

Enough said. But to resume, last night before I came back I decided. Come come. After the six hour slog in the kitchen, with a few soiled banknotes in my pocket alongside a wad of raw mince I demanded in place of the customary charred burger, I was persuaded by the lyric poet to attend a celebration. After work, he said, play. A certain talent for concision there, no doubt about it. This being all the persuasion I required, we set off with glee in our hearts. After all one seldom has the opportunity to play. Enjoy yourself as they say, you're only young once. I mean were. And certainly for some time now I have felt the compulsion to revert to play. But I have been unable to do this, having forgotten how to in the first place. How even to begin to play. Because you have to begin in order to go on, that's obvious. But I make a mess before I start, before I pick up a brush. Because the canvas in my mind is not blank, far from it. I tell you it's choc-a-bloc with the method I intend to employ and the end result I intend to achieve. Which isn't play at all, on the contrary it's work. But let's press on with the story. Last night at a party, I met a woman. How to describe her? Come to think of it why bother, the important thing to grasp is that a certain sort of eye contact occurred. So there I am with an open if nonverbal invitation to explore the mysteries of the emotions etcetera and what do I do? Nothing, not a word do I utter in response to her fervent enquiries. And you know why don't you? Because even this was work, work from beginning to end. Not that there was a beginning, not that it had an end. But I was silent from exhaustion, from the fatigue of that first question she asked: *What do you do?*

I digress most surely.

As if it were possible to do otherwise given the irrelevance of the entire preamble. Preamble to what I would like to know? A preprandial preamble, that's the point. I must get the dinner on somehow before boxing day is upon us. The dead hamburger meat is still tucked safely away there in the coat pocket. It may not be a festive meal, however. However perhaps a sprig of holly, but no. There is nothing wrong with mince no matter what day of the year it is. Many less fortunate would give their testicles for a steaming hot plate of christmas mince. And you cannot beat it for consistency. For that matter versatility is the great thing about mince, it is international in a way in which turkey is not. The Greeks the Italians the Chinese the Americans the French, where would they be without mince? Each of these diverse peoples has come to an understanding with mince. It is a common denominator among men. Of course to make myself a hamburger would be something of a busman's holiday, but I see no reason not to go Greek or Italian. Admittedly either would require condiments I do not possess, but then imagination must be the main ingredient in any work of art. One can draw on experience as the meal proceeds. You could always go and wish old Mrs Bernard next door a merry one, she might invite you in for a slab of her suet dumpling. That would surely do the trick. Think of all the many errands I have run for her when her arthritis has been playing up. Two ounces of spam and the People's Friend, such dreadful privation. Or the Normans on the other side, I'm sure they'd be only too pleased to have a starving artist on this day of the feast. Somebody to share the nut roast and hollyberry yoghurt with. But where is everybody, in the name of God? What a black bleak bloody deadend street. What's the matter with you all, don't you know that we're mortal!

I am what I do when I'm alone.

I am not alone after all despite everything all things considered. Because a light has just gone on over the road. I stood by the window, watching it with grateful eyes. I saw a red haired woman moving about in her kitchen. Even tried waving but the bitch didn't wave back. Why should she wave back I would like to know? But what is it coming to I ask you when two solitary christmasers can't even give each other a bit of a wave through the driving snow? Maybe if I strung myself up, I could hang myself from the light fitting there, maybe then she'd wave. Self-crucifixion would be better all the same. I knew I would put that easel to good use one day. When I was standing there at the window, I saw my own reflection in the glass. And suffering christ what a specimen. Old newsreels of refugees sprang to mind. Must have scared her out of her wits to see such a creature waving at her from its window. Moreover, as I stood there waving and seeing the rough beast in the glass, a revelation came to me.

Dawn is breaking.

There is no doubt that contrary to all my heartfelt convictions it has been getting lighter, not darker at all. Even now another light goes on in the cul-de-sac and another, each throwing into silhouette a scrawny bit of fibreglass and tinsel. Dingdong merrily on high, a conspiracy begins to happen around one. Whole bedfuls of pyjama-clad children erupt into excited laughter. Little boys rip the lids from long boxes to reveal the glittering weapons. Mrs Bernard presents her cat with a tin of salmon. And I expect the Normans are exchanging presents also. More legwarmers darling how thoughtful. Enough of this selfpity I say, stuff the lot of them. Here I stand, my own man. And you should be thanking your stars the family didn't invite you this year. At last they've accepted the idea that you don't show up for the annual slaughter. No wonder, the last time I went there was that senile old uncle of an in-law telling you over his turkeybreast why he never got married. Premature ejaculation for crying out loud, O the miserable pity of it. Worse than a suffering circus with all those dogs and cats and nephews under the table. I have no desire to partake of the family gathering again, believe me. But this dawn breaking on me like this when I believed it to be night is something of a reversal. This means that it must be seven or so in the morning, and that I have slept two hours at the outside. No wonder I feel like hell. But I should make the most of this, it's a rare opportunity to get started early. Started on what? Begin.

O no not this again.

But yes there is no doubt about it, they've started downstairs. I can hear them through the floor, the young couple with the five year old and the alsation. That door that bangs and bangs like a dead fullstop. Between their heavy sentences. Doubt if they talk in sentences, who does a grammarian maybe. Kill anything off with good grammar. Hack the living disorder of it all into the subject verb object and what have you? A carcass, correct. Nail it down there with the semi-colons, make sure it doesn't run away. People declare their love like that after all. I the subject, love the verb, you the object. Make love like that too sometimes, I am speaking from experience. Whereas mess is mess and you can't get away from it. Listen to them down there though, christmas morning or not, bawling blue murder at each other already. Makes you grateful for your solitary despair I can tell you. To smell one's own armpit a veritable privilege. Their silences sound worse than the bouts of language. Always throwing the same verbal shit at each other anyway. His voice like a moaning trombone, saying opprobrium opprobrium. Hers a violin practice fit to shatter decanters, accusing accusing. Needless to say the alsation provides the rhythm section. Then the brat trying to get a scream in edgeways, enough to make a grown man weep. That's married bliss for you, till death do us etcetera. All this coming up between the floorboards on a daily basis you understand. A moment of sanity when the brat laughs aloud, voice clear and sound as a trumpet. Then a bang and the trombone blares its fury, the violin squeals like an electrocuted cat. The alsation murders what shreds of peace remain. The poor little bastard is wailing again, endlessly and inconsolably.

To be born into this barnyard.

I had to escape. I put the mince on to sizzle, no onion but nonetheless sustenance. I took to my heels for a hearty preprandial constitutional along the canal bank. Though I have a keen eye for nature I espied no rat. Instead, though it is hard to believe, there were a couple of swans. With the canal iced over here and there too, this mythical pair doing figure-eights in the slime and showing off the lengths of their necks. One felt obliged to stand and watch despite the freezing wind, though of course they ignored me pointedly. Different if I'd had a bit of bread to throw, a different story then no doubt. Can't say I took delight in their stylish curves or whatever, but one of them stepped up on the bank and I saw her feet. She was wearing galoshes it looked like. Nor can I honestly maintain that I enjoyed contaminating the virgin white which lay on all sides, some bastard had been out before me walking a dog. I returned forthwith to find the aforesaid mince dried to a frazzle. Which I ate nonetheless with gratitude. Now the day is in full swing around me. The door downstairs has girned open and I hear the mother saying to her son, Get out there and make a snowman.

The christmas spirit.

There he goes into the cul-de-sac, kneedeep in the nothing. Still blubbering but beginning to realise his freedom. Away from the menagerie of that home of his. He wipes off his snotters on his sleeve. Looks round at it now, all this nothing that's landed in the cul-de-sac. He kicks the nothing, picks it up and throws it at itself. He sits down on it and starts to scoop some of it into a pile. Something begins to emerge from the nothing. That's the idea, a snowman. I am down to it at last, scratch I mean. The blank canvas in the mind. No postponing it, this is it. Shoulder to the wheel, nose to the grindstone. Already he begins to emerge, the absence of his face. The shoulderless form, lacking ears fingers toes. From the many shades of white he shall emerge, moronic and oracular. An abominable snowman, and believe me he will be abominable.

Here goes.

The Hunter of Dryburn

YEZ'LL HAVE a drink.

Whit izzit, a pinta heavy izzit? A pinta heavy. N whitzzat yer young lady's drinkin? Hullo darlin, aaright? Aaright. Gin an tonic izzit? Gin an tonic it is. No problem friend, Ah insist. Pinta heavy na gin an tonic. On me.

Yez dinnae mind me talkin tae yez, dae yez? Mean dinnae get me wrong, ken whit Ah mean, mean Ah'm no meanin anythin or anythin. Mean Ah'm no tryin tae chat ye up or nuthn sweetheart. No tryin tae chat up yer burd or nuthn son, aaright son? Aaright. No me, naw.

Naw but is soon is yez walked through that door Ah could tell. Ah could tell yez were in love and that, the paira yez. Stauns oot a mile so it diz. Na could tell yez were educatit people ken. Na could tell yez wernae frae roon aboot here, that wiz obvious. See it's no very often Ah get the chance, mean tae talk tae folk like youz in here ken. Ah enjoy a bitty intelligent conversation ken. So Ah sez tae masel, whit wid the Auld Man adone? He's deid ken, death by misadventure. Yez probably read aboot it in the Evenin News. So Ah sez tae masel, the Auld Man widda bought these young people a drink, had a bitty conversation ken. See the Auld Man wis like that ken. Friendly. Hospitable pal, you've said it. Unless he didnae like the look o somebody, then he wisnae quite sae hospitable.

So yez took the wrong road frae the motorway, ended up in sunny Dryburn? Jist thought yez might as well pop in for a quick wan, fair enough. Is soon is yez walked through that door Ah sez tae masel Aye, they've probly took the wrong road frae the motorway. Quite frankly like, if a thought for wan minute yez had come in here deliberately like, Adda tellt yez tae get yer heids looked. See Dryburn? Sa dump.

Tell ye this hen, you're beautiful so ye are. Naw seriously. Nae offence son, aaright? But Ah mean how diz a boy like you get a beautiful wummin like that? It beats me, so it diz. Nae offence son, aaright?

Aye Dryburn's a dump aaright. Mean yez can see that for yersels. Mean it's no whit ye'd caa a village even. Mean, whit is there? Thirz haufadizzen shoaps. Thirz a chip shoap. Thirz the church and thirz the chapel. An thirz four pubs. Five, if ye count the hotel up by the motorway. See folk used tae pass through here a loat before thon motorway. Nen there used tae be a station up by the steelworks. Thats where he worked, the Auld Man, afore he deed. Shut doon noo though, the steelworks. Yez widda liked tae meet the Auld Man, no that he went tae Uni or nuthn but. But he wis an educatit man ken, ayewis wi a book in his haund. Edgar Allan Poe, Ernest Hemingway, you name it. Ah've been readin a bitty this Ernest Hemingway masel ken, story boot shootna lion. Ken the wan Ah mean darlin? That's it son, that's the wan.

Aye he's a great writer right enuff. An thirz a helluva loata good advice aboot huntin an that in this story. Course it's aa aboot a place in Africa or somewhere like that, jungle an aa that ken, no a place like Dryburn. Whit's that yer sayin sweetheart? Aye it looks aaright frae the train right enuff, but sa dump. See the trains used tae stoap in Dryburn afore they shut doon the station ken. It used tae be mair o a community ken. A mean, no a community exactly but. But at least ye could get a train oot o the bliddy place. See the Auld Man wis a respectit person in Dryburn. Yez probly read aboot him gettin killt, in the Evenin News it wis. Aye. Mean he wisnae like a doakter or a lawyer like, but folk looked up tae him ken cause he wis educatit. Educatit hissel so he did. Used tae sit in that coarner there, in his wheelchair ken, and poke folk wi his stick and tell them tae mind their fuckin langwitch. An folk pyed attention tae him tae. See everybiddy went tae him wi their payslips, Ah mean if they couldnae work oot their tax or their superan. Or like if somebody had tae go up tae court, they ayewis went tae him tae find oot their rights, ken. It wis like they consultit him aboot anythin like that. That's right sweetheart, you've said it: he wis a walkin Citizins Advice Bureau. Except he couldnae walk much ken, cause o his legs.

He had it up here see, the Auld Man, he could work things oot for folk. Take numbers for instance, he wis a wizard wi numbers. Mean if somebody had a win on the horses ken, the Auld Man could tell them exactly, doon tae the last haepenny, exactly how much they'd get back, minus the tax an everythin. Naebody could touch him at poker. Or dominoes. A wizard, he wis a wizard aaright. See noo that he's deid there's naebody else like him left in

Dryburn, naebody who can tell folk how much o a tax rebate tae expect ken. Except mibbe me. See that's why Ah've startit tryin tae educate masel a bit ken, that's why Ah'm talkin tae youz educatit folk like, so Ah can mibbe learn somethin frae yez.

Tell ye somethin son, ye're bloody lucky so ye are. Beautiful wummin like her, don't try an deny it.

So Ah'm readin this Ernest Hemingway tae try and educate masel a bit ken. See me and the Auld Man used tae go in for a bit o huntin wirsels, up by the Union Canal. Course, there's no very much tae hunt roon aboot here. Nae lions an tigers, ken? But there's a helluva loata rats up there at the canal. Hundredsa big dirty great rats. Ah wonder if Ernest Hemingway widda done the same, Ah mean if he lived in this area. No much else tae dae in Dryburn except hunt rats, take ma word for it. Mibbe he'da enjoyed it, ken, then he'da come in here wi me an the Auld Man efter a guid night's huntin an had a few pints wi us. Aye, right enuff son, it wid be Absinthe if he wis buying. Here that wid gie Louis, the barman owre there, that wid gie him somethin tae think aboot. Absinthe by christ. See Louis used tae take a rise ootae us when we came in here wi the guns ken. 'Here come the big game hunters!' he'd say, or: 'Bag any tigers the night boys?' He wis ayewis at us aboot it ken, then wan night the Auld Man shot him. Yez shooda seen Louis' face. Yez shooda heard the lang-witch in here that night! Ah mean he wisnae hurt or nuthn, the pellet jist nicked his airm. Course, the Auld Man said it wis an accident ken, said he wis jist pretending tae take aim ken an the thing went oaf in his haund. Yez shooda heard Louis, talk aboot wild! He wis gonnae bar the baith o us, but he needed the custom ken. Louis stoapd pullin oor leg aboot it efter that, Ah can tell ye.

Ever shot anything son? Naw? Ye dinnae agree wi it? So how come ye like readin Ernest Hemingway, eh?

Skip it son.

Ah gave it up anywey, efter the Auld Man deed. See that's how he goat killt in the end. Yez musta seen it in the News, quite a scandal so it wis. Well, we were up there oan the canal bank wan night, ken, jist sittin watchin the ither bank. It wis near the railway bridge up there, ken? Yez've probly seen the canal frae the train. That's where ye get the rats. So there we were, me an the Auld Man, jist waitin, when who should come along but two well-known members of the local constabulary, ken?

Mean Ah ken it's no nice, shootin rats, it's no very nice, but if ye've read Ernest Hemingway ye'll ken aa aboot the waitin bit. It wis the waitin bit that wis guid — like fishin, ken? Nuthn in the canal tae fish for though, that's why we got the guns in the first place. We didnae talk much, me an the Auld Man, when we were waitin for the rats. Naw, we jist liked sittin there oan a nice night, wi the sun oan the water an aa that, waitin. So along came this pair and startit askin us questions an aa that. The Auld Man jist sat there sayin nuthin, so Ah did the same. See, he wisnae a very talkative person unless he felt like talkin, an he never really liked talkin tae the polis. He widnae say somethin unless he had somethin tae say, see whit Ah mean? Aye, you've said it son, laconic. The Auld Man was laconic as hell sometimes. An this was gettin up the polis's nose, the wan who wis askin aboot the guns and what not. Nen the ither wan says, An what exactly is is ye're plannin tae shoot in any case? Nen the Auld Man says: Vermin. Jist like that, Vermin. Oh, so it's vermin, is it? says the first wan, the wan askin aa the questions, an then he says somethin aboot us bein vermin wirsels. Nen it transpires they want us tae haund owre the guns there an then. See it wis when wan o them tried tae take ma gun that it startit. A fight. Now, can Ah ask ye tae tell me, honestly, do Ah look like a violent person? Do Ah, tell me straight? Naw, Ah'm no violent. Well, hardly ever. But it wis like when ye're wee, in the playground at schuil, an somebody bigger than ye tries tae take away yer luck-bag, ken? That's whit it wis like — Ah jist saw red. So there wis a bitty a scuffle oan the canal bank, ma gun went oaf an wan o them got a pellet in the neck. Then the coshes, ken? Ah wis strugglin wi baith o them when Ah realised the Auld Man wis in the canal. He'd went right under. Probly he tried tae get in among us wi his stick, ken? An he musta got pushed intae the water. Ye can imagine whit it wis like. Ah couldnae swim tae save masel, neither could the Auld Man. So the wan withoot the pellet in his neck had tae strip oaf an dive in. Ah remember the ither wan sayin, Let the auld bastard drown! By the time we got him back up oan the bank, he wis deed. So that wis that.

A tragedy, the paper called it. Course, Ah wis up in court for resistin arrest, assault an aa the rest o it, but the judge wis lenient cause o the Auld Man an that. Whitzat hen? Ring a bell, does it? Think ye mibbe saw it in the News? Aye, it's likely.

Sorry tae be sae morbid an that.

Thing is, Dryburn's no the same place withoot the Auld Man.

Ah blame masel for whit happened. Ah shoulda had mair sense than tae start a scrap wi the polis. So Ah'm tryin tae educate masel, see, so Ah'll be able tae help folk decode their pyeslips an that.

Tell me somethin before ye go, friend. What's yer honest opinion o Ernest Hemingway as a writer? A ken he's a great writer an aa that, but earlier the night Ah wis readin that story aboot shootn the lion, and Ah donno. Ah couldnae be bothert feenishin it. Ah came doon here for a coupla pints insteed. It's no Hemingway's fault ken, it's ma fault. Ah wis enjoying the story an everythin, till it gets tae the bit aboot the kill ken. Cause the trouble is ye see, Ah jist cannae imagine the lion. Ah jist cannae picture the lion in my mind, know whit Ah mean? Aa Ah can imagine's a rat, a dirty hairy great rat. A rat's no the same thing as a lion, somehow.

Yez'll be on yer way, then. See, it's no very often Ah get the chance tae talk tae educatit people like youz. Ah wisnae tryin tae chat ye up or nuthn sweetheart, aaright? Aaright son? Ah wisnae trying tae get aff wi yer burd or nuthin son. See Hemingway? See if he did live in this area, in Dryburn like, he'da probly left years ago an got hissel a joab as a journalist.

Ah'll tell ye somethin else while yer lady friend goes tae the toilet, son. It's no very often we get wummin like her in here. Nae offence, but she's quite a catch. Quite a catch, Ah'm saying. If ye want ma advice, haud ontae her. Or somebody else might, believe you me.

Ah'm no meanin anythin or anythin, but ye're a jammy wee swine so ye are and don't you try an deny it.

Hiss

QUIET IN HERE, isn't it?

Very quiet and peaceful.

Of course they'd want it to be, wouldn't they? If you listen closely though you can hear something, always something. Some little fly roaring past on its motorbike. I can hear something now, if I listen closely enough. It's faint though, very faint. It's a faint sort of hissing sound, that's all it is, a faint hiss.

Unless I'm just imagining it.

But I don't think I am, no, I can hear something all right, always something. I have to listen closely, of course, very closely to be able to hear it. And even then, even then it's by no means distinct. It's by no means easy to identify what this hiss is, where this hiss is coming from, what the source of the hiss is.

It isn't coming from you, is it?

I just got back, from the East. Better late than never, eh? I can hear you saying, 'Where the hell's fire have you been?' That's what you always say, isn't it, when I get back from somewhere, 'Where the hell's fire . . .', that's what you always said. It was a long flight, I can tell you. Had to change planes in Moscow. Couldn't leave the airport though. I was hoping to get some kind of transit visa, visit Lenin's tomb, send you a postcard. A postcard from Moscow, you'd've liked that. But I couldn't leave the airport. The airport was nice though, very nice. Compared to Delhi airport it was a palace. I don't know about these Russian air-hostesses though, they're not very glamorous. Why should they be glamorous? That's what you'd say. You're right. They didn't smile either, when they came round with the water. They came round with cups of water. They were a bit abrupt about it all, I must say. Why shouldn't they be? You're right, why shouldn't they. I suppose you could say they were refreshingly ordinary, like the water, refreshingly ordinary and abrupt. I suppose you could say it made a change to be openly despised by the hostesses, yes, I for one felt very like a lackey of Imperialism. Mind you, they did invade Czechoslovakia in 1968. We fell out about that, you remember, hardly spoke a word for weeks. We never really agreed about anything after that, did we? You'd've liked a postcard from Moscow though, pity. Of course, it wouldn't be here yet. I'd've been back before it. Better late than never though, eh?

No, it can't be coming from you.

It must have a source, of course. Every sound has a source, but sometimes it's difficult to say what the source is, that's all, even when you can hear the sound quite clearly. Even then, sometimes, depending on a number of variable factors, it can be virtually impossible to say with any certainty what the source of any given sound is. Especially in a strange country, of course, in an unfamiliar environment, when you've just arrived, and it's late at night, and you're exhausted because you've been travelling for days. Take Thailand, for instance. You wouldn't want to go to Thailand. Prostitution, Americanisation, corruption. After the flight to Bangkok I took a train, then a bus, then another bus. Then a ferry, then a motor-boat. After the motor-boat I got a lift on a cart, an ox-drawn cart. It was a remote island, very remote. The old man with the cart didn't speak much English. Just a few words like 'dollar', 'mark', 'pound sterling'. So I got out the phrase book. I'd bought it in Bangkok. So I tried to ask him about a place to stay. A difficult language though, if you pronounce a word the wrong way it can mean something different. So there I was asking about a hotel, but for all I know I was probably asking him to measure me up for a coffin.

A coffin is a complete waste of good quality wood. I must say, I'm inclined to agree with you there. I bet they whip the bodies out before they cremate. It would make sense in a capitalist society. Sell them over again, make a fortune.

No hotels on the island, as it turned out. Not even a guest house. Nothing. The old man with the cart motioned for me to climb in. So there I was, on the back of a cart among the sacks of rice and a load of old stinking fish, going two miles an hour along this little road through the jungle. He took me to a place I could stay in. It was a hut. He owned it apparently. He gave me the key and told me in sign language to lock the door before I went to sleep. He took some money. Before he went away he pointed to a little village further along the coast. I could get something to eat there apparently. Then he went through the business with the key again, telling me to lock myself in before I went to sleep.

When I asked him why he pointed out to sea, then up into the jungle, then he made his hand into the shape of a gun. He finished off this little mime show by drawing his finger over his throat. Of course, I'd heard about the pirates in that part of the world. Vietnamese guerillas apparently. You'd know more about them than me though. Anyway, I was too tired to worry about being raped and looted, so I gave him his money and he left. There I was, the sea stretching out in front of me, the jungle behind me, in a hut.

Maybe it's coming from the lights. I must say, they've made a good job of the lighting in here. I suppose you could say it's quite tasteful. It's certainly subdued, I'll say that for it. And yet it isn't too dim. It must be a strip-light of some kind, concealed behind those louvred panels. It isn't too bright, or too dim, and you can see why they wouldn't want it to be either. They'd want it to be inbetween, to achieve a subdued effect. Presumably that's the effect they were trying to achieve and I must say they've succeeded completely.

I couldn't sleep though, because of all the noises, all the sounds outside the hut. I thought it'd be quiet there, very quiet and peaceful. It just hadn't occurred to me that the jungle would be noisier than the city at night. I just lay there listening, listening to all the sounds. Some of them I could identify, of course. The sea. Dogs howling in the village. Cicadas. But there were other sounds I couldn't identify, sounds I'd never heard before, sounds for which I could imagine no source. And these were the ones that kept me awake. Things rattling, squeaking, screeching, hissing . . My imagination was running riot.

No, it can't be coming from the lights.

I could hear everything quite clearly, of course, because the walls were made of some very thin stuff, strips of dried palm leaves I think, patched together, crosswise, like a basket. That's what it was like, like being shut inside a basket. It was hot inside that basket. I could hardly breathe. After a while I started to nod off, then I heard something. I didn't know what it was, but it sounded very strange. It seemed to get louder as I listened to it. At first I thought it was some kind of wild animal prowling around. Then I thought there were more than one of them, a pack of them running around somewhere out there. It took me a while to realise that it was motorbikes, the roar of motorbikes coming closer. I couldn't tell how many there were, not even when they all roared up and stopped outside the hut. The light of their headlights came in through the basketwork walls, long needles of light. Then they put the lights out, and the engines stopped revving. Even the jungle seemed quiet then, very quiet and peaceful. After a while I could hear their voices though. Whispering, either whispering or shouting. They seemed to be arguing a lot, whoever they were. I had no idea what any of them were saying, of course, no idea whatsoever. The voices sounded urgent though, as if they were very serious about something. I thought I heard one of them laughing, then I wasn't sure if it was a laugh or the sound of someone being strangled. I was sitting up on the bed by this time, out of my sleeping bag, listening. Then suddenly the voices stopped. I remembered the cat then, taking the cat to the vet's in a basket. I suppose I was beginning to feel the way the cat must've felt. I kept thinking somebody was going to open the lid of my basket, then I'd have to jump out and make a run for it. Then they started with the lights.

It could be the air-conditioner. They must have an air-conditioner in here somewhere, because they've obviously gauged the temperature very deliberately. They wouldn't want it to be tropical. Not too chilly either, they wouldn't want people shivering. It's pleasantly cool, that's what it is. They've done it all very tastefully, I must say. Those lights behind the louvred panels, I must say . . .

They were flashing them, their headlights, at the hut. On and off, on and off. Needles of light through the walls. I was trapped inside the basket. And all these needles of light coming in . . . The points of them seemed to congregate on my body, all the little points of white light. They looked like glow-worms, crawling over me, contracting and extending their tiny lengths as I breathed. It went on for hours like that, with the headlights flashing, and the glow-worms, and the breathing, and the jungle, and the heat. They wanted me to go out. They wanted me to unlock the door and go out. It was a kind of torture. After a while I started to hear something else, a sort of thudding sound, like somebody running round the hut. but it was too loud for that, too close. It sounded as if it was coming from inside the hut. I couldn't identify it, you see, I couldn't determine the source.

You'd've preferred Moscow.

I suppose I must've been eight or nine years old. The cat kept wailing and howling all the way there. Everybody on the bus kept looking at me. And when it was my stop, I picked up the basket and saw the wet stain underneath. It couldn't understand what was going on around it, you see. It could hear the sounds — the screech of the brakes, the roar of the engine, the voices — but it couldn't identify them. On the way back from the vet's, with the empty basket on my knee, that's when it really started. Not with the invasion of Czechoslavakia. Why did you make me take the cat to the vet's to be put down, Dad? Couldn't you have taken it?

I didn't unlock the door though, I just sat there on the bed, in the basket. I waited for them to go. They went away just before dawn. I don't know who they were, or what they wanted. I'll never know. But after that I kept on hearing the noises, all the strange noises outside the hut, and inside the hut, inside me. It took me a long time to realise that the thudding sound was me, it was my heart. I can still hear it, like somebody running. I have to listen closely of course, very closely to be able to hear it . . . It's even fainter than the hiss.

In some places they play pleasant music, to lull the deceased into their eternal slumber. I suppose that would put paid to the hiss . . .

It must be the air-conditioner.